PRAISE FOR LOREN D. ESTLEMAN

"The American West endures in the Western stories of Loren D. Estleman through his portrayal of the characters who made up the West."

- THE BLOOMSBURY REVIEW

"For readers who can't get enough of Elmore Leonard and Ross Thomas, try Estleman. He's that good."

- PEOPLE

"...Estleman goes on my short list of the peer group I can read for pleasure—along with Dutch Leonard, Robert Parker, and Ross Thomas."

- JOHN D. MACDONALD NEW YORK TIMES
BESTSELLING AUTHOR

"Estleman rivals the finest American novelists with his gritty vision and keen ear."

- THE WASHINGTON POST BOOK WORLD

THE BANDIT AND OTHER BEST WESTERN STORIES

THE BANDIT AND OTHER BEST WESTERN STORIES

LOREN D. ESTLEMAN

WOLFPACK
PUBLISHING
— EST 2018 —

The Bandit and Other Best Western Stories
Paperback Edition
Copyright © 2024 (As Revised) Loren D. Estleman

Wolfpack Publishing
1707 E. Diana Street
Tampa, FL 33610

wolfpackpublishing.com

Paperback ISBN 978-1-63977-660-3
eBook ISBN 978-1-63977-659-7

CONTENTS

HARD BONE AND RED BLOOD

AN INTRODUCTION BY EDWARD GORMAN AND BILL PRONZINI

The air had a snap to it, the vapor of our spent breath at sundown was as thick as milk, and in the morning we had to use our gun butts to knock loose the ice masks that formed on the horses' faces as they slept.

The Stranglers

He has written meticulously researched historical Westerns, an incisive history of the Western novel, hard-edged crime fiction, articles on Sherlock Holmes for scholarly journals and two book length Holmesian pastiches. His 1984 mystery, *Sugartown*, is regarded by many as the best traditional private eye novel of his generation; similarly, his 1987 novel of the events following the famous gunfight at the O.K. Corral, *Bloody Season*, is regarded by many as the best historical Western of his generation. He has won major awards in both the Western and crime-fiction fields: a Best Novel Spur from the Western Writers of

America for his account of the life and death of Wild Bill Hickok, *Aces and Eights* (1981), and a Best Short Story Spur for "The Bandit" (1986); and from the Private Eye Writers of America, a Best Novel Shamus for *Sugartown*.

Loren D. Estleman has done all of this—and more—before quite reaching his thirty-sixth year.

He was born in Ann Arbor, Michigan, on September 15, 1952, and has lived in that area all his life. He received his early education at Dexter community schools, and matriculated at Eastern Michigan University in Ypsilanti, where he earned a B.A. in English and journalism in 1974. He worked as a reporter for the *Ypsilanti Press* in 1973; as editor of the *Community FotoNews* in Pickney, Michigan, 1975-76; as a special writer for the *Ann Arbor News,* 1976-77; as a staff writer for the *Dexter Leader*, 1977-80. Since 1980, he has been a full-time writer of fiction.

One forms two quick impressions upon meeting him: that at one time he must have boxed (he did) and that he may perhaps be shy (he is). He is also self-effacing and soft-spoken—so soft-spoken that there was once a standing joke among the clients of his former literary agent, Ray Peekner, now deceased: "What is the quietest sound in the world? Loren and Ray having a talk." And yet he is the holder of iron-bound opinions on many topics, including writers and writing, which he has been known to defend at considerable and eloquent length. One should never praise Max Brand in his hearing, for instance, nor should one ever refer to Westerns as "cowboy stories"; it is his belief, and rightly so, that anyone who uses that phrase has contempt for what is not only a vital literary form but the only truly American one.

His first novel, *The Oklahoma Punk*, a gangster saga set in the turbulent years of Prohibition and the Great Depression, was published in 1976. He followed this with his two Holmesian pastiches, *Sherlock Holmes vs. Dracula; or, The Adventures of the Sanguinary Count* (1978) and *Dr. Jekyll and Mr. Holmes* (1979), and with his first Western novel, *The Hider* (1978). *Motor City Blues*, his first of eight mysteries featuring Detroit-based private investigator Amos Walker, appeared in 1980.

In a scant dozen years, he has published twelve Western novels, fifteen crime novels (three others are concerned with the violent exploits of a former Detroit mob killer named Peter Macklin), one book of non-fiction (*The Wister Trace: Classic Novels of the American Frontie*r, 1987), and more than forty short stories, articles, and essays. And yet, for all his prolificacy—and despite the fact that he eschews modern technology, preferring to do all his writing on a 1923 Underwood manual—he is a careful, polished writer and a tireless researcher who believes in maximizing the realism of his work.

A strong argument can be made that as a writer of historical Westerns he is at the apex of talents; that Western fiction is his one true metier. In his dozen novels in this field, he has accomplished the difficult feat of imposing on the traditional Western story both an absolute realism and elements of the parable and other purely literary devices to create an amalgam that is uniquely his own.

The sentence from *The Stranglers* which forms the epigraph to this introduction is typical of Estleman's style. It contains all three elements of the very best descriptive writing: clarity, idiosyncrasy of phrasing, and memorable imagery. But finely honed narrative prose is not the key ingredient in his work: nor are such other virtues as his ear for dialogue, especially the rhythms of frontier speech, and his ability to write action tersely and with originality of expression. It is realism. Story, setting, character, voice—all are unerringly real.

Encomiums for *Bloody Season* from two of his contemporaries give further testimony. Douglas C. Jones, author of *The Court-Martial of George Armstrong Custer and Elkhorn Tavern*, says that this novel, "probably comes closer than anything ever written in revealing not only event and character but mood and atmosphere in Tombstone, Arizona Territory, 1881...there is no myth here. It is hard bone and red blood, as real as the barrel on a Frontier model Colt pistol." And Elmore Leonard, writer of best-selling crime fiction and of such memorable Western novels as *Hombre*, states that Estleman's account of the aftermath of the O.K. Corral gunfight "is the best one I've ever read. It's high drama with a documentary ring that draws the reader into every scene. I mean you're *there*. It's so real you can even smell the horses." Estleman himself has this to say about his Western writing:

At its best, my style is highly visual, and depends upon exterior description to elicit a subjective opinion from the reader. Whether a character is to be thought of as wicked or heroic or comical or otherwise is up to my audience to decide based upon what I have shown them of his appearance or behavior. Nowhere in my work will you find a passage wherein the narrator turns face forward and says, "He was an evil man." If that fact isn't on the face of things, I've failed. Needless to say, this reticence on my part to present my own opinions upon a given subject or character has led to some involved and not always civil discussion with editors. I expect this and bear them no ill will because of it. Amiable concurrence does not good art make. Nevertheless, the tightrope between subtlety and incomprehensibility is one I prefer to walk rather than plunge into the ephemeral depths of the obvious.

Four of Estleman's twelve Western novels are narrated by a Deputy United States Marshal named Page Murdock: *The High Rocks* (1979), *Stamping Ground* (1980), *Murdock's Law* (1982), and *The Stranglers* (1984). At once these are fast-paced, violent, suspenseful detective novels with frontier Montana and Dakota Territory settings; historical novels peopled by actual persons, either by name or in fictionalized incarnations; sociological studies; and within the framework of their times, morality plays.

As for Murdock, he is anything but a standard Western-fiction hero; rather, he is as complex and contradictory as any living human being—dedicated and imposing, yet amiable, and in subtle ways both vulnerable and compassionate.

Estleman's nonseries Western novels can likewise be read and enjoyed on more than one level. *The Hider* is an adventure story and the tale of a boy's rite of passage, achieved on a hunt with a buckskin-clad old drifter for the last surviving buffalo in the Oregon of 1898. *The Wolfer* (1981) has a similar theme: an eastern writer joins an aging wolf-hunter on a search for a wolf of legendary reputation. There is considerable comedy—and considerable pathos as well in *Mister St. John* (1983), the story of Irons St. John, unsuccessful candidate for the Missouri House of Representatives, failed real estate promoter, failed businessman and husband, whose only real talent is manhunting and who—with the aid of a not-so-adept Indian tracker, a half-blind sharpshooter, and a Sunday school preacher wanted for murder—sets out to recapture some of his past glory. In *This Old Bill* (1984), which Estleman considers his most accomplished novel, he again separates fact from legend in a surprising and moving chronicle of the life of a famous frontiersman, in this case Buffalo Bill Cody. And in *Gun Man* (1985), he tells the grimly realistic tale of a Great Plains shootist as such men's lives were lived, not as they are commonly portrayed in lesser novels and films.

None of these full-length works is conventional in its development or its telling.

Each, in Estleman's hands, is something special.

The same special quality applies to his short fiction. First-rate novelists do not always make first-rate short-story writers (and vice versa); one reason, speaking metaphorically, is that the novel is a long journey which may be approached with cursory planning and undertaken with a great deal of spontaneity and extra baggage, whereas a story is a brief excursion that requires more precise planning, a careful itinerary, and a minimum of baggage. Estleman understands this better than most writers and proceeds accordingly.

Inasmuch as the market for Western short fiction is severely limited these days, he has written but a few stories; all appear in these pages for all are worthy of inclusion. Some with criminous elements were first *published in Alfred Hitchcock's Mystery Magazine,* where many of his Amos Walker short stories have been printed; a few originally appeared in anthologies, another in the semiprofessional magazine *Pulpsmith;* two are published here for the first time; two are the intended opening chapters of *The Wolfer* ("The Pilgrim") and *Mister St. John* ("Young

Mister St. John"), excised before publication for editorial reasons; and one is a self-contained excerpt from *Bloody Season* ("Kate"). Each may be termed a novel in microcosm, which is to say that it is a full-bodied story containing every important element of a good novel. The best of them are near-perfect Western miniatures.

There is Estleman's first published short story, "The Tree on Execution Hill" (AHMM, August 1977), an odd little tale filled with hints of a social-political-historical philosophy that are likely his own. There is "The Pilgrim," with its rich historical cadences and vivid images: "Directly overhead, a sky the color of mildew hung so low it seemed to cast its shadow over the dull snow upon which the shelters lay scattered as if cast by a gambler's hand." There is the taut action of "Mago's Bride," the grim wisdom expressed by Page Murdock in "The Angel of Santa Sofia," the Faustian and supernatural elements of "Hell on the Draw." There is the splendid fusion of mystery and history that marks "Bad Blood," "The Pioneer Strain," and "Rossiter's Stand." There is the flawless structure of his Spur winner, "The Bandit," with its equally flawless descriptive simile: "His beard was yellowed white, like stove grime." And for good measure, there is Estleman's brief but penetrating essay, "Beds and Bullets: Sex and Violence in the Western Novel," which further reflects his personal attitudes toward frontier and Western fiction.

Here, then, is The Best Western Stories of Loren D. Estleman. Here, then, are some of today's finest tales of the American frontier, by a young writer whose future evocations of the past will surely be even more profound.

THE BANDIT AND OTHER BEST
WESTERN STORIES

THE CAT KING OF COCHISE COUNTY

People in Salt Lake City called Chickenwire Chickenwire on account of the device he'd come up with to keep chickens from being eaten by Elder Evilsizer's boar, Deuteronomy.

The business had started when Sister Gertrude, the Elder's primary wife, had fed the carcass of a hen to the hogs because she wasn't sufficiently certain of what had killed it to cook it and didn't feel like digging a hole. The hogs, particularly old Deuteronomy, discovered a taste for chicken, and after that whenever a bird strayed near, the last images its pea brain carried to Pullet Paradise was of the boar's hairy snout and gnashing teeth. Feathers, bones, beaks, and claws were all grist for Deuteronomy's mill; often only a furious pattern in the dust of the barnyard and a pepper of blood remained to tie up the mystery of the diminishing local chicken population.

It wasn't long before the aging swine's dietary preference led it to neighboring farms, which was the reason a committee of whisker-faced, sad-eyed Mormons showed up at Chickenwire's mercantile store to ask him for some miracle that would protect their best layers from the predatory pig. Shooting the offender was out of the question. So, too, was demanding that Elder Evilsizer take measures to keep his boar at home where it belonged. The violence of the elder's disposition, compounded by his reputation as one of the last of the Destroying Angels involved in the Mountain Meadows Massacre, was legend, preventing any word or action on the part of his gentler neighbors that might call down his wrath.

Chickenwire's response was to fashion a net from spools of wire he had rescued from a wagon abandoned by Western Union in the Shoshone country north of the Great Salt Lake. He reasoned that by stretching the screen around skates encircling the birds' scratching ground to keep Deuteronomy out, and above their heads to keep the chickens in, the farmers might put an end to the bloodshed without inviting retaliation.

The theory proved sound. The wire was bought, the pens built, and the pig, after a number of unsuccessful attempts to breach Ilium, was forced to settle for the turnips in its trough, together with such game as it could find out on the great alkali plain.

Moreover, the idea turned out to be an invention that outlasted its original necessity.

Months after Deuteronomy got hold of a bad prairie hen and finished its existence on the Evilsizers' dinner table, orders for the remarkable wire continued to stream in.

There were still wolves and stray dogs to contend with, and the participating Mormons' many wives had reported a secondary benefit in being able to cross their yards without dragging their hems through fresh droppings. Chickenwire, whose vision was not always equal to his entrepreneurial spirit, had reason when he parted with his last thirty feet to regret not commandeering the entire wagonload when he'd had the chance.

When he came to think about it, however, he thought perhaps it was just as well he ran out when he did. The wire was devilish to work with, having slashed up a dozen pairs of leather gloves he'd hoped to sell at a profit, and he was confident that as word got around that his store was no longer a source of the stuff, the farmers would stop calling him Chicken-wire. Born Michael Aloysins McDonough, he had been known as Iron Mike in the California gold camps, where he'd made his grubstake knocking down miners for wagers. He much preferred that address; although the thirty years since he'd given up prospecting and come to make his way as a Gentile among the Latter-Day Saints had packed forty extra pounds around his impressive musculature, he still introduced himself as Iron Mike.

He'd liked the raw life of the camps. Successful

man of commerce that he was, he missed the rough company and unpredictable nature of a place that could double its population almost overnight once a major lode was uncovered, or lose a citizen in a heartbeat when the same card turned up twice in a poker game in one of the tents. Most of all he missed the candor. The Mormons were much like everyone else as to percentages of good and bad, but altogether too civilized for a man who liked to know right off what sort of person he was dealing with. In the camps you knew where you stood. If a man didn't like you he came at you with something, fists or a shotgun or some kind of club. In Salt Lake City he mouthed pleasantries to your face while spreading stories behind your back that the flour you sold contained rat poison.

It was fitting, then, that Chickenwire McDonough's vague dissatisfaction with his current circumstances should be turned into action by a man from the camps.

From the moment the fellow entered the store, some two or three weeks after the last ten yards of wire had been sold, it was obvious he was no Mormon. His beard was too scraggly, for one thing—more the result of late unfamiliarity with a razor than deliberate cultivation—and his filthy slouch hat, sun-blanched flannel shirt, and torn overalls were as far from the sober Black that the faithful wore to town as one could come. He read aloud from a list scribbled in thick pencil on a greasy scrap of paper he held close to his sunken, red-ringed eyes. They were the items that a man traveling a long distance would request: axle grease, flour, cartridges, iodine for cuts and fistulas, beans, brogans, coal oil, and four sacks of Arbuckle's.

"Homesteading?" Chickenwire totaled the order in his ledger.

"Prospecting." The stranger's vocal cords grated against each other like hacksaw blades. "Bound for Montana and silver."

"I hear silver's growing scarce up that way."

"I don't care. It's too cold there for rats and that's good enough for me."

"Rats?"

"They're big as rabbits in Arizona. Had me a nice little claim a day's ride out of Tombstone, but the rats run me out. I can put up with lice and Apaches and highwaymen, but I sure don't warm to waking up with a large gray rat chewing on my big toe."

"Can't you trap them?"

"Not the ones in Cochise County. They're too smart for traps. Some of 'em's smarter than either one of my partners. I sold out to them finally and hauled my freight north. My partners, not the rats; though they're big enough to do their share of the digging, and that's a fact."

"The cats down there must be lazy."

"Not lazy. Scarce. Cats go with barns. Ain't no barns down there, nor farmers to build 'em. Just miners and Mexicans. Mexicans don't keep cats."

Chickenwire ran broken-knuckled fingers through his whiskers. "How's the dirt?"

"Rich as Vanderbilt. The Can-Can Restaurant sells ham in champagne sauce. Two bucks a throw, and they run out every Saturday. Them nuggets don't get time to knock the dirt off on their way to some fancy man's pocket in town."

The prospector paid for his supplies in silver and carried them out. Chickenwire never saw him again, and in time forgot his features. But what he'd said changed the merchant's life.

When young Lemuel Dent reported to the mercantile the next morning for his part-time delivery duties, he found the proprietor gummy-eyed from lack of sleep but sparking with energy from some unknown source.

"How many friends you got, boy?"

Lemuel considered. His employer was perched on his stool behind the counter with a brand-new ledger flayed open before him. The pages were black with figures and the countertop was a litter of short chewed yellow pencils. It was obvious he'd been doing sums all night. At inventory time, Chickenwire's temper was shorter than his pencils, and a thing to tread carefully around. "I don't know," answered the boy; and because that didn't seem specific enough be added, "Some."

"Round them up. There's a quarter in it for you *if* you can have them here by noon."

Youthful avarice flared in Lemuel's eyes, slightly

crossed since an encounter he regretted with a mule's left hind foot on his tenth birthday. "What do I say?"

"Tell them there's money to be made."

In the boy's absence, more than one potential customer found Chickenwire's door locked and the CLOSED sign in the window. Had they been able to peer around the shade, they'd have seen the storekeeper removing slats from his inventory of wooden crates and replacing them with scraps of wire formerly deemed too short to mess with. By the time Lemuel rapped at the door, accompanied by eight of his closest friends and one or two boys he didn't like at all, Chickenwire had finished nine of a projected twenty cagelike contraptions, complete with doors hung on leather hinges and secured with tenpenny nails on the sliding-bolt principle.

Mopping his great bony brow with a smeared bandanna, the proprietor surveyed this bounty of boys barefoot and brogan-shod, overalled and knickerbockered, dirty-faced and scrubbed pink. At length he grunted his approval and ostentatiously surrendered a disk of shining silver to the young man responsible, who pocketed it without ceremony. This transaction was observed closely by his companions, who then looked to Chickenwire for their share in the bonanza.

"A fifth part of that," he announced. "Five cents, if you don't know your fractions. A nickel I will pay for every stray cat you lads bring to me between now and sundown. A dollar extra to the young fellow who delivers the most. *Healthy* cats, mind. I'll not pay for mange or palsy. Fly, now!"

The command provoked a thunder of feet and a brief scuffle on the threshold as a number of lithe bodies attempted to pass through a single doorway at the same time.

What occurred in the streets between midday and dusk on that date has achieved regional immortality as the Great Cat Hunt of Salt Lake City, and requires no extrapolation here. Suffice it to say the next day's Deseret News reported two discharges of rock salt by homeowners at undersize prowlers vaulting over back fences with wailing felines clamped beneath their arms, and one close call involving a dray wagon when a skinny youth in corduroys dived in front of the horses to snatch a flying Siamese. By the time these and similar incidents were connected with the increased demand at apothecary shops for iodine to treat cat scratches, and the whole traced to their source, Chickenwire McDonough had crossed the territorial line, unaware of the animus against him.

In his defense it must be stated that when the day was done and the merchant found himself, among the noisy multitude, in possession of two cats wearing collars and bells, he instructed the boys who had brought them to return them to their owners: "Stray cats, I said!" The rest he paid for. The promised bonus went to Fatty Ambrose, whose corpulence did not prevent him from depositing no fewer than seventeen cats in the mercantile's back room.

The tally, once the boys had been ushered out with pockets jingling, came to forty- six, including thirteen tabbies, ten calicos, seven black witch's familiars, six tigers, one blue Angora, and nine hollow-flanked alley veterans of indeterminate color and pattern. Reluctantly—for he calculated their collective worth to be sixty dollars—Chickenwire released six cats by way of the back door, two per cage was crowding things well enough, and he needed to eliminate as many casualties due to disease and fights as possible during the long journey ahead.

Every inch of which, he reasoned, would prove well worth the inconvenience.

For if the miners around Tombstone were content to part with two extremely hard- earned dollars for a dish of plain barn swimming in fizzy wine, how much would they pay on a one-time-only basis to be rid of the rats that plagued *their* digging and made their lives miserable in the tents when they slept? Ten dollars hardly seemed unwieldy.

Thus, upon an initial investment of three dollars and twenty-five cents for inventory, plus an approximate fifty dollars to outfit himself for the trip, which would be covered six times over when he sold the store and its stock, Michael Aloysius McDonough stood to gross four hundred dollars at the end of the frail—far more than the amount required for a place to live and a healthy interest in a claim that showed promise. The adventurer in him embraced both the odyssey and the camp camaraderie for which he pined; the speculator in him warmed itself at the fire of the riches that would be his.

Elder Evilsizer, six feet four inches of fierce, white-bearded piety with a back as straight as a Winchester barrel, heard out Chickenwire's proposition the next morning from the bentwood rocker on his front porch an hour's ride from town, where he was accustomed to keeping an eye on his hired man to ensure he plowed a straight furrow and avoided his secondary wife's rose bushes.

"Two hundred dollars," he said. Chickenwire shook his head. "Three hundred is the price, and a bargain at that. I have nearly a thousand tied up in the building and stock."

"Two hundred dollars."

The conversation continued in that vein for some minutes, at the end of which Chickenwire, no longer a storekeeper, drove away from the farm with twenty ten-dollar bank notes in his inside breast pocket. The sum was a disappointment, but the elder was the only member of the community who could put his hand on more than a few dollars at a time. Most of the others traded in chickens and homemade quilts.

Although he considered his own delivery wagon, a medium-size Studebaker designed for use as an ambulance by the federal army during the late war, more than adequate for his excursion, Chickenwire gave the blacksmith down the street from the store thirty dollars to replace a doubtful spring and rein-force the tires, axles, and hounds with iron. While that was being done he fed the cats, changed the shelf paper he had placed in the cages to collect waste, and organized the necessaries he had excluded from his transaction with the elder to carry him a thousand miles. Among these the item that consumed the most space was sardines—nearly a hundred tins packed in oil to sustain both him and his cargo. Casks of water, a bearskin for protection against the arctic blasts that sometimes occurred even in the desert, repair tools, and medical stores completed the kit. This last precaution came to mind while he was scratching a bothersome new itch, turning his thoughts toward witch hazel and the like.

The wagon was ready the following day. He loaded his supplies carefully, distributing the burden equally so that the construction would not pull against itself while lurching over uneven ground. He hitched it to a fine chestnut and bay he had taken in trade for an overdue bill owed by a farmer who had gone bust on the worthless ground west of the lake, and stacked the cages atop one another in the bed, lashing them securely. The cats, cranky from captivity and sensing more unpleasantness ahead, screeched and hissed and tried to claw him through the wire. And then he was on the seat and away, without once turning to look back at the enterprise that had supported him for close on three decades.

Allowing time for delays, he calculated the trip

would take a month to complete. In the jockey box were railroad survey maps of the Utah and Arizona territories. Behind the seat, within easy reach, he had placed a Springfield carbine for shooting antelopes and jackrabbits when he tired of sardines, and a Walker Colt for shooting Indians and highwaymen when they tired of local prey. The very thought of hazard set his blood to singing. He marveled that he'd stuck out city life as long as he had.

———

Three cats died the first week.

He blamed himself for the first, a moth-eaten tabby whose bones showed, but whose ravenous appetite and nasty disposition had convinced him the animal was heartier than it appeared and worth bringing along. After three days it stopped eating. On the fourth morning it was as cold and stiff as jerky. Then a pair of cage mates, a black and a calico, got into a savage fight, and although Chickenwire separated them by moving the calico in with the dead tabby's cage mate, the torn and bleeding combatants took infection and perished within twenty-four hours of each other. He cast out the carcasses, cleaned both cages, and used them to relieve the crowded conditions elsewhere. Thirty dollars shot to hell.

The itching he'd noticed back in Salt Lake City had by this time turned into an angry rash on his neck and between the fingers of both hands. Despite the application so far of half bottle of witch hazel, it kept him awake nights in his bedroll and stung like bees when he sweated in the heat of the day. His eyes had become puffy, too, and uncontrollable fits of sneezing plagued him for an hour after he fed the cats or changed the paper in their cages. Although he knew nothing of allergies, he was no fool, and immediately connected this sudden breakdown in the aggressive health of a lifetime to his furry charges. But he had stood worse for much smaller rewards. Come Tombstone he would be shut of the business.

He found the Fremont River three times wider than on his last crossing. Unseasonal rains in the Wasatch Mountains had made a mockery of its banks and accelerated its current, uprooting small trees and dismantling century-old beaver huts as if they were built of playing cards. Circumventing it would take him three days out of his way.

While he felt he could put up with the itching and sneezing for the extended period, he was not as confident of the cats, two more of which were off their feed. Chickenwire tied one end of a hundred-foot length of hemp to a rock on the bank, unhitched the horses, swam the chestnut over with the other end of the rope in hand, and made it fast to a fir tree on the opposite bank. He then worked his way back, hand over hand along the rope, swam the bay across, and worked his way back again. After two hours' rest he spent the remainder of the day caulking the wagon.

When that job was finished he wanted desperately to make camp, but he feared the river would continue to swell throughout the night and become uncrossable by morning, leaving him stranded with his horses on the wrong side. He double-fastened everything, taking special pains with the cages, and, standing in the wagon bed up front, grasped the rope with one hand and pushed off with a shovel. The current snatched greedily at this fresh flotsam, trying to turn it downstream, but using the shovel as a paddle and gripping the rope until his fingers cramped, Chickenwire guided the wagon toward the opposite bank by force of his own might.

Halfway across he felt the shovel slip and nearly fell overboard as he lunged to retrieve it.

The river tore the handle free and took it away, the spade end ducking and bobbing until it was out of sight. Lest he follow, he grasped the rope in both hands, inadvertently creating a pivot. The rear of the wagon swung around, a corner dipped beneath the surface, the cargo shifted, and one of the leather harness straps that held the cages in place burst with an ear-splitting report. The top cage toppled off. Chickenwire, struggling to maintain his grip on the rope, watched helplessly as the cage containing two cats splashed into the water. The doomed animals squalled piteously; and then they, too, like the shovel, were beyond seeing.

The sudden absence caused a change in balance that brought the swamped corner up out of the water.

Now the captain of the craft allowed the current to push it the rest of the way around and, sliding his hand along the waterlogged hemp, worked his way to the stern, which had now become the bow. He took with him the Springfield carbine. Leaning over the tailgate, he lowered the wooden stock into the water to act as paddle and rudder. Five minutes more and the submerged wheels came to rest against the original bank. He laid aside the carbine, leaped out, and with the river eddying around his hips, exhausted his remaining strength hauling the wagon up the slope and out of the Fremont's clutches.

In blue twilight he lay in the sparse grass on the south bank, soaked to the skin, caked with mud, his chest heaving and his heart hammering in his ears. He was sure it would stop. When it didn't, when his breathing slowed and he found he could move his limbs more than an inch at a time, he dragged himself to his feet and proceeded to assess the damage.

The wagon and its surviving contents had come through remarkably well. In addition to the cage, he had lost a water cask, and a case of rifle cartridges, and two sacks of flour had become saturated. Some of the pegs holding the wagon together had loosened, but he was sure he could tap them tight with the blunt edge of his axe once they'd dried. The lost cats were the tragedy. One was the blue Angora, a beautiful, sweet-tempered female he'd hoped to palm off on some sporting lady with a soft heart and deep pockets for twenty dollars and recoup some of his losses.

However, he was a practical businessman who knew that every venture carried risks. If just half his cargo came through, he stood to realize a seven thousand percent return on his original investment—more than enough to satisfy any plunger, let alone one interested mainly in arranging a comfortable stake for mining. And so when the cats and horses were seen to and his bed prepared, dreams of avarice claimed him until the sun hit him in the face like a skillet.

In his charge was a particularly obstreperous tiger, a slat-sided alley fighter with one eye, a broken tail, and an ear that drooped from a lacerated muscle, who, unlike most of the others, had refused to adjust to the confined quarters. From dawn to dusk it spat and sprayed, and at feeding time swiped a set of claws nearly an inch long at the hand that opened its cage. Chickenwire bled copiously until he fell into the habit of pulling on a pair of the leather gloves he had used to work with the wire. More than once he had considered releasing the disagreeable creature to starve in the desert, but there were many miles to go and the value of each item in his inventory was climbing.

Instead, rearranging the cages to restore balance, he placed the tigers in the corner left vacant by the incident in the river. Should history repeat itself, the sacrifice would not leave him inconsolable.

Arizona offered no obstacles until the Colorado River, an unfordable torrent that made the Fremont seem a sleepy creek by comparison. There a weather-checked little ferryman loaded with big-handled pistols under a sombrero wider than his shoulders walked around the wagon, evaluating its features and cargo, and offered to take him across for twenty dollars.

"I never paid more than a dollar to cross water in my life!"

Quick as thought, the little man drew both pistols and thumbed back the hammers. The weight of the barrels bent his wrists. "Then I reckon you best do your business this side."

Chickenwire chewed his whiskers, then paid over the requested amount. Halfway across the charging river, propelled by an ingenious lock-lever device attached to the guide rope, the little man stopped the ferry and demanded the rest of his passenger's poke.

"You're holding me up?"

"I got expenses," said the ferryman. "What good's your stake if you can't get across?"

"What good is it if I don't have it at all?"

Out came the pistols. "I done my talking, mister."

"I don't have it on me. It's in a false bottom in this cage. I'll get it." Chickenwire undid the latch on the top cage.

"Back off! How do I know you ain't got a hogleg bid out there?"

"That's foolish." He started to open the door.

"I'll blow you into Mexico if you don't back off!"

Chickenwire stepped back, raising both hands. Belting one of the pistols, the ferryman covered him with the other and swung open the door. The tiger cat pounced. Cursing, the ferryman snatched his hand back, bloody. Chickenwire stepped in, knocked aside the pistol, and threw a left hook from as far as the gold camps of California. He felt the ferryman's jaw give way and caught the pistol as he fell. He slammed and latched the cage door and pointed the pistol at the man groaning on the deck. "Can you swim?"

"What? No!" The ferryman was supporting himself on one hand and trying to hold his jaw together with the other.

"Pity." Chickenwire laid the pistol inside the wagon bed, lifted the man beneath the arms, and pitched him over the rail. The big sombrero could still be seen riding the whitecaps long after its owner had gone under. Watching it, Chickenwire wished he'd thought to take back his twenty dollars.

He lost the best part of a week detouring around the Grand Canyon, whose size he had greatly underestimated, whipped the horses brutally over the San Francisco Mountains to make up the time, and sweated off twelve pounds crossing the desert west of San Carlos. Three calicos, a black, and an alley mongrel perished in the heat.

The buzzards that perched in the mesquite bushes near his camp had grown too bold to frighten off, even when he fired at one with the Springfield and sent it dashing to the ground. He wasted no more ammunition on this project, there being more birds than he had shells.

The rash had spread over most of his body. When a sneezing fit came upon him he was forced to alight from the wagon and lead the horses, putting as much distance as possible between himself and the cats. Nothing else would bring relief.

It was during one of these intervals that he encountered his first Apache.

The suddenness of it took his breath away. He had been directing his eyes to the ground to avoid the glare of the sun, and when he raised them the Indian was there, straddling a rattle-boned paint not fifty yards in front of him. The man was naked but for a breechclout and high-topped moccasins and carried a long-barreled rifle slung behind his back from a strip of braided rawhide. His eyes were fissures in a face the color and apparent texture of the pottery bowls that the merchant used to accept in trade from the tame Shoshone who had come to his store for supplies. This, however, was no tame Indian.

Instinctively, Chickenwire dropped the reins he was holding and lunged toward the wagon and the Springfield behind the seat. The seat exploded. He lost his balance and sat down hard in the sand. The Apache, having unslung and fired his rifle in less than a heartbeat, was already seating another charge, ramming it home with a thin wooden rod as long as the barrel of the ancient flintlock. It was ready to fire again before Chickenwire could regain his footing.

He stood with his hands clear of his sides as the Indian heeled his paint up to the wagon.

Up close, the newcomer appeared to be younger than the white man had thought at first. His eyes, graphite-colored, glittered between narrowed lids as they took in every detail of the wagon and its owner. At length he stepped down and, making it clear that he would raise and discharge his weapon at the first sign of resistance, inspected the horses in their traces, examining their teeth and haunches and squatting to feel their fetlocks.

Rising, the Indian pointed to the chestnut, then his own horse, repeating the gesture several times. Chickenwire stared doubtfully at the paint, which looked even bonier close up and moth eaten besides, but nodded, observing that even an outmoded firearm was of enormous advantage in horse trading. He unhitched the chestnut and accepted the horsehair attached to the paint's bridle.

The Indian showed no inclination to leave. Waving the white man away from the wagon and the rifle inside the bed, he walked to the rear and peered inside. For a moment he contemplated the strange cargo in silence. Then he reached inside, fumbled with the latch on one of the cages, opened the door, and pulled out a yowling black by the scruff of its neck. Now he grinned for the first time. Guessing his intent, Chickenwire took a step in his direction. Immediately the flintlock came up. The grin vanished.

Chickenwire stopped, raised his hands high. He watched as the man swung aboard the chestnut, expertly checking its attempts at rebellion with his knees as he slung the weapon over his shoulder and forced the cat into a reclining position, head down across the horse's withers. Then he wheeled, uttered a high-pitched cry, and was gone, galloping toward the horizon with his long hair flying unfettered behind him.

The puzzle of the cat's value to the Apache occupied the merchant's thoughts for a long time afterward. Companionship? An ingredient in some tribal ritual? Food for the family tepee? At which point he sought a better subject.

The paint proved a bad trade. It had never been broken to any kind of wagon, and when its new owner attempted to maneuver it between the traces, it fought the bridle and tried to rear. When he dug in his heels, the horse arched its back, causing a sudden slackening in the reins, then rocked back on its hind legs and clawed the air. Ducking to avoid a slashing hoof, Chickenwire lost his grip on the reins. The paint spun and clattered away in the direction its late master had gone. In another minute only a cloud of dust remained to mark its passage.

This was not a good turn. Chickenwire was stranded in desert country with a wagonload of cats and a tired bay unequal to the burden.

He jettisoned everything that wasn't absolutely necessary. Axes were superfluous in that landscape, where buffalo chips served for firewood. Coffee, bacon, and flour were luxuries when sardines sufficed, weary though he had grown of them. Toiletries, tobacco, a fine old walnut rocker his grandfather had made and which had accompanied him all the way from his Ohio birthplace—out everything went. Doubling up the more compatible cats allowed him to discard a number of cages.

The load was still too much for the bay. When the animal stopped and hung its head after barely a dozen yards, Chickenwire raged, stamped about, and tugged at his beard until the roots popped. Then, as in a trance, he hoisted five cages to the ground and unlatched the doors. Nine cats bolted in nine directions. Despite his distaste for the noisy, irritating creatures, he hoped they would find enough roadrunners and pack rats to sustain them.

When the tenth cat did not emerge from its cage, he looked inside. One of the muddy-colored beasts of mysterious lineage lay licking a moist, pink, mouse-sized squirm with a squinched face. Two more were huddled inside the curve of the cat's body, sucking energetically at teats.

Chickenwire's face felt funny. He realized he was smiling—beaming, for the first time in recent memory. Enormous as were the odds against three kittens surviving the journey, he looked upon the miracle as a sign of hope. He secured the door and gently lifted the cage back into the wagon. Now he altered his plan to toss out a full case of sardines after releasing the cats and saved out a dozen tins. Mothers required more food.

New life does not greatly improve a grim situation. Not counting the kittens, he was down to half his inventory, with a wagon that was still too heavy unless he climbed down and walked beside it at regular intervals, and better than a hundred miles to go before Tombstone and the Promised Land. And he had a fresh scratch on his hand courtesy of the scrappy tiger, registering its disapproval at the prospect of a roommate after all this time. Already Chickenwire regretted his softhearted decision not to abandon the tiger to the desert with the others as a reward for helping out with the larcenous ferryman.

The monsoons caught him shortly after crossing into what he determined to be Cochise County, home of Tombstone and an area larger than some European countries. The rains transformed the earth to ropy mud that sucked the wagon down to its hubs, slowing him to a crawl and obliging him often to step into the vacant harness next to the bay and pull with all his might when it stuck. At night he lay shivering in his bedroll, coughing up specks of blood, still sneezing and itching but too weak to scratch.

A kitten died. Two grown cats succumbed to pneumonia. He shared that malady and was certain that before long he would share their fate. Still he pressed on.

When a second kitten died he shed tears, but he

wasn't sure whether they had more to do with genuine sorrow or his runny eyes.

Huddled in his soaked covers beneath the wagon, he dreamed Death came to him. Deep in the folds of Death's black hood shone the yellow-green eyes of a cat. Late into the next day he resupine and swaddled. The sun was low when the plaintive meowing of his famished charges aroused him. His skin felt cool. The fever had broken.

After two days he felt strong enough to continue. In the meantime a calico had succumbed. He disposed of the carcass, moved its cage mate in with another, and threw out the empty cage. Resigned now to tragedy, he looked in on the mother and remaining kitten, and was surprised to find that both were doing well. The young one seemed even to have grown. Rather than encouraging him, however, the news found him numb. He was past all emotion.

The rains stopped. Almost immediately he longed for their return. He could actually see the puddles turning to steam, the earth drying and cracking like old plaster. He had not been out of his clothes in weeks; his own caked sweat grated beneath his arms and behind his knees. When he treated himself to a swallow of water from his suddenly dwindling supply, the liquid stung his weather-checked lips like acid. Despite reasonable rationing among the cats, two more calicos and a tabby dried up and died.

He wondered what the next generation would make of the derelict cages along his trail.

Three days from Tombstone, he came to an arroyo that stretched to the horizon in each direction. It was steep and strewn with boulders, but he calculated that going around it would cost a week, with nary enough water left in his casks to sustain a man for half that time, much less a man and thirteen and a half cats. Gripping the brake lever to control the descent, he gave the reins a flip.

The bay picked its way over rocks of unequal size and loose shale, making gasping snorts as the wagon lurched behind, threatening to throw it off balance. A third of the way down, the animal lost its nerve and stopped. Chickenwire, who could feel rubble shifting beneath the wheels, cursed and smacked his whip at the horse's rump. It whinnied, shook its mane, and took another step.

A piece of shale the size and shape of a bishop's hat turned under its hoof. A knee buckled. The wagon lunged.

Chickenwire released the brake and lashed the whip, shouting at the top of his lungs. The bay bolted.

When the wagon's left front wheel struck a boulder, the merchant heard wood splinter. He was standing at the time and threw himself clear as the wagon heeled over and skidded on its side into the lead, pulling the screaming bay down the slope all the way to the base. Cages flew. The yowling of the terrified cats echoed in the arroyo for a full minute after the dust had settled. Dazed, Chickenwire lay listening as the horse's cries grew feeble and finally stopped. When at length he tried to push himself up, his wrist bent suddenly, shooting white heat to his shoulder. He didn't know he'd passed out until he opened his eyes and saw a pair of caked boots inches in front of his face.

"You dead, hoss?"

They were the first words he'd heard since the encounter with the ferryman. He made a reply, but his throat was parched and it came out a dry rattle. Boots squatted. Pain lashed Chickenwire again as his arm was lifted and probed from elbow to hand.

The man smelled of sweat, earth, woodsmoke, and bacon. "That's as broke a wrist as ever I seen, hoss."

He raised his voice. "Syke, fetch me that busted shovel and a canteen."

He was turned onto his back. A hand supported his head as he swallowed a blessed draught of mossy-tasting water. While Boots fashioned a splint from a splintered wooden handle and a length of hemp, Chickenwire observed that the arroyo was alive with men in filthy Levi's and flop-brimmed hats—miners, if he remembered his camp days at all—calling information to one another from their positions next to the ruined wagon and scattered cats. He learned the bay was dead of a shattered spine and that most of the cages were empty, having broken open on impact and freed their captives. Three contained dead cats.

"What about the rest?" he asked.

The man called Syke, shorter and stouter than the horse-faced Boots, returned from the wagon, mopping the back of his neck with a red bandanna. "Six in the wagon, and one don't look too good. And a kitten, though I wouldn't count on it lasting. The mother's dead."

"Dutch Bill's got him a goat," Boots said. "He might could get it to suck goat's milk from a neckerchief. Don't know what your plans was, hoss, but we sure can use cats in these here parts. We got more rats than prospectors."

Chickenwire made a decision. "Take them."

Boots's eyes rolled white in a face stained with silver clay. "This here's a problem. It ain't nothing to josh about."

"I'm not joshing. You saved my life. I'll need a horse, too, and water and provisions to get me to town. Divide them up how you want. If I never see another cat it will be too soon."

The miners moved swiftly, as if afraid he'd change his mind. Within the hour a gentle dun mare was produced, complete with a worn saddle and pouches filled with tins of beef and tomatoes. Boots helped Chickenwire straddle the mare and hung a canteen on the horn. One of the other miners, an honest lot, had found the merchant's poke and brought it to him.

From his high seat Chickenwire surveyed the wreckage of the wagon and its contents. "Help yourself to whatever you can salvage. I've had my life's portion of sardines, as well."

"Good luck to you, hoss," Boots said. "My chewed fingers and toes sure do thank you."

That night, thawing the evening chill from his bones before a fire and trying not to think about his throbbing wrist in its makeshift sling, Chickenwire pondered his future. The remainder of the money the elder had paid him for his store in Salt Lake City, while not enough to buy into a good claim, might net him a partnership in a store in Tombstone. In a year or two he might set a sufficient amount aside to invest in pay dirt.

The enterprise would be a success after all, and it would not depend on cats. After all those weeks in their company he could still hear them meowing.

Meowing.

He caught himself looking for the source of the fancied sound and smiled. The tinkling of the pianos in the all-night saloons would drown out the echoes soon enough. He would find the cure for his rash in the arms of a sporting lady. Chickenwire was picturing the enameled women in their bright dresses when a specter came into the firelight and slunk toward him, meowing.

He sneezed, and the fresh pain in his arm made him curse. The cat—for it was the one-eyed, vile-tempered tiger he had despised for a thousand miles

—shrank from the oath, hissing and flattening its single undamaged ear; then started forward again.

Obviously, the beast had been among those that had escaped when the wagon overturned. How or why it had trailed him to this spot didn't concern him. The species filled him with rage. With his good hand he reached for the Walker Colt under the saddle he was using for a backrest, cocked it, and rested the barrel atop his raised knee, sighting in on the tiger's chest.

"Cat, you just went and spent the last of your nine lives."

Ignoring the weapon, the animal came forward the rest of the way. At his knee it paused and ducked its head, rubbing its body against his leg. As it did so, a velvety rumble issued from deep inside its throat. The sound caught a little from a lifetime of disuse.

Chickenwire said, "Well, I'm damned," and let down the Colt's hammer gently.

Early Tombstone cherished its characters nearly as much as it did its heroes and villains. Well into a new century, when old-timers wearied of recounting the exploits of the Earps and Clantons and Johnny Ringo, they would wet their whistles and launch into the story of how itchy McDonough, part proprietor of the Golden Gate Mercantile on Fremont Street, came to town with nothing to his name but an old mare and his one- man cat, Elder Evilsiz.

THE BARBER

Alberto Pacifico reckoned himself the best barber in Teamstrike.

This was no small boast. In its three short years of existence, the Colorado goldtown had acquired no fewer than eleven barbers, in addition to nineteen saloons, fifteen dry goods stores, four churches, two bathhouses, and thirty-six houses of ill fame—though to put the truth to it, nearly half of the last were not houses at all but tents, and twelve of those were just wagon sheets under which the women slept who worked in the other twenty-four, and took home work. As the fields were far from mined out, there was no reason to expect there would not be much more of everything, barbers included; but Alberto Pacifico was sanguine. He would be better than all of them.

His was the twentieth generation in his family to take up the tonsorial profession. The first Pacifico,

Franciscus by birth, had trimmed the august head of Theodosius I, and been granted the hereditary designation Pacificus by that emperor for the calm and steady hands with which he sheared and anointed the imperial scalp. Alberto had five brothers, all of whom worked in prestigious parlors throughout Europe. He alone, the youngest, had journeyed to the New World that he would not spend his life in his brothers' collective shadow.

In New York City he had fared poorly. The place was full of barbers, and living was expensive. The money he had brought with him would not pay the rent on his own shop if he intended to go on living in even his tiny walk-up apartment above a steaming laundry that parboiled him in summer and made him feel clammy all winter. The barber who ran the shop where he found employment was a butcher whose poor skills turned away customers, as well as a martinet who would not let Alberto try out his best cuts on those who could not afford to frequent a better shop. When an excited customer who said he was on his way to the Colorado goldfields showed him an article in Harper's Weekly about the rude life in the mining camps, Alberto had looked at all the unshorn heads in the steelpoint engravings and decided Colorado needed him a lot more than Manhattan. He turned in his apron, took his pay (minus the customary kickback to the ward boss), and invested it along with the little he'd managed to put aside in a train ticket to St. Louis.

Now, dusting his growing collection of shaving mugs, he remembered as little as possible of the months of peasant labor unloading riverboats while he'd saved for a wagon, team, and supplies to take him to the Rockies. The rough camp he'd found waiting for him demanded only a tent, a lantern, and a straightback chair to set up business. The local prostitutes at least were happy to see a barber in town; there wasn't a one of them who didn't have to use most of her face powder to cover razor burns, and they had vermin enough in their ticking without the lice that were so attracted to heads of long shaggy hair. Alberto owed his first two dozen customers to the cajoling of the whores. He'd brought a case of Bay Rum, whose sweet limey freshness transformed the thousand-and-one stenches of life among the prospectors. Soon there was not a man in camp who would remove his hat in the presence of a fille de joie unless his hair was properly plastered down with tonic and pink skin showed around his ears. After a month Alberto had abandoned his tent for a cabin built of freshly felled timber. At the end of the first year, the Napoli Tonsorial Parlor moved into a respectable frame building constructed of materials provided by Teamstrike's first sawmill.

By then there were other barbers in town, but none with his reputation. His equipment was also the best. His razors were Sheffield steel with custom ivory handles imported from England, and no monthly mail packet arrived from St. Louis without half a dozen china mugs packed in straw, bearing the names of frequent customers lettered in gold. Last spring he had sent all the way to San Francisco for a Union Metallic Chair with adjustable back and revolving seat, the first of its kind in the territory; customers fought, literally battled with fists and feet for the privilege of a shave and a trim in the reclined comfort of its green plush upholstery. It was the pride of Teamstrike, a thing spoken of in the same hushed breath with the bonanza.

First come, first served was the rule at the Napoli, with one exception. At ten a.m. Tuesday and Friday, Alberto Pacifico reserved his chair for *the* Honorable Nestor *Goss,* judge of the miners court and owner of the Lucky Lucy, the richest claim in Colorado, one hundred sixty ounces to the ton in March of 1868 and still producing. A big man when he came to the fields, sidewhiskered and shaggy-browed, Judge Goss had grown enormous on ham in champagne sauce and strawberry shortcakes at the Golden Rule Restaurant and now hired others to descend into a shaft that would no longer accommodate him. Indeed, the generously spaced arms of the Union Metallic pinched his buttocks and its cast iron frame shuddered beneath his weight.

Alberto spent as much time with his bottles and brushes as any artist. As he caressed a creamy lather out of the cake of glycerine soap in the judge's mug-- the handsomest one in the rack, with the putative Goss family crest rendered in enamel and gold on the side--he plied his customer with questions about the brick house he was building on a hill west of town. The barber was considering erecting a new and bigger shop, and was curious about the cost and benefits of brick. So intrigued was he with the judge's answers that he failed to take note when the shooting started in the street.

The discharge of firearms was nothing new in Teamstrike. In fact, on a day early in the previous June, when the sun managed to rise and fall without a single report overheard inside town, the editor of the local newspaper, christened The Mother Lode, had thought to mark the event with a column on the front page. Thus it would be unfair to hold the barber accountable for ignoring yet another set of explosions as he applied a hot towel and then lather heated to body temperature to the judicial cheeks and chin.

It happened that Floyd "Rat" Brennan, a prospector noted more for his capacity to imbibe strong spirits than his skills with pick and shovel, had fallen out with Oscar Johansen, the bartender at the King Midas, over a matter of short change. The argument spilled out into the street, where Brennan produced a Colt's Thunderer and fired, missing the bartender's head by inches but killing instantly a twenty-year-old mule named Flo. Flo was the property of Tiny Hardaway, who left off loading the buckboard to which the mule was hitched to take up the shotgun he kept under the driver's seat.

At this point the fighting became general.

Bystanders with grudges against the principals unlimbered various items of ordnance, and for two or three minutes the muddy street between the King Midas and the Napoli Tonsorial Parlor reminded more than one veteran of the field at Shiloh. By the time order was restored, the casualty count included a mule, deceased, a nasty flesh wound in Toby Bragg's left buttock, the plate glass display window in the Rocky Mountain Gentlemen's Emporium, and one dead judge.

Alberto blamed the Honorable Nestor Goss's fate on misplaced official indignation.

The barber had finished with his customer's admirable sidewhiskers and was negotiating the tender bit below the right ear with his best razor when a stray bullet burst the china globe on the newly installed oil streetlamp in front of the shop. The judge, who in a characteristic flare of civic pride had financed the new lamps out of his own pocket, gripped the arms of the chair to hoist himself upright and demand an end to the disturbance. A steady hand is no match for an agitated subject. No amount of cotton gauze, witch hazel, and pulverized yarrow can staunch the bleeding from a jugular. Although Albert cried for help, and help arrived swiftly in the shape of a dozen miners for whom a good turn done Teamstrike's wealthiest citizen meant seed money for a promising new shaft, Judge Goss expired quickly in a sanguinary wallow.

A coroner's court was convened quickly, during

which it was firmly established that the deceased had lost his life due to misadventure. No one blamed Alberto. Deacon Heppelmeier made sonorous and sincere mention of "a tragic accident" during the eulogy preceding the tramp to Cemetery Hill, and passing mourners patted the barber's shoulder to indicate understanding and support. They acknowledged that the same thing could have happened to any of the town's eleven barbers. And they stopped coming to the Napoli.

At first Alberto charged the steep drop to normal hesitation. Miners were a superstitious breed, and could not be expected to hop into a chair whose upholstery was still damp from industrious soaking and scrubbing to remove all traces of the life's blood of its most recent occupant. At the end of the first week, however, the barber became concerned; and *when* the monsoons came and still no customers showed up for a trim and a scrape to lift the depression caused by skillet-black skies at noon and relentless downpour, he realized that none of his neighbors was willing to expose his scalp and throat to a barber who had presided over the untidy death of a rich and popular resident. Had the victim been some anonymous drifter, or one of the many ragged prospectors upon whom fortune and geology had refused to smile, the situation might have been different; but if a moneybags like Goss was not safe, what chance had an ordinary miner?

One evening, a month after the tragedy, Alberto

was seated in the splendid chair, chin in his hands and his brain sunk into a mulch of self-pity and undesirable alternatives, when the door opened and a gaunt, black-bearded face thrust itself inside. The apparition wore a hat with a drooping brim and an oilskin poncho streaming water. A pair of red-rimmed eyes sought out the proprietor in the light of the Chesterfield lamp.

"You Pacifico?" The voice, scratchy as if from disuse, made a hideous business of the pronunciation.

"Yes, sir!" said Alberto, stepping down eagerly to fetch his razor and scissors; for here was a man desperately in need of expert barbering.

"Thought so." The short ugly snout of a shotgun came up from under the poncho and belched fire.

But the barber's reflexes were better than the man's aim. Alberto flung himself to the floor just as a fistful of buckshot struck the Chesterfield lamp, spraying a geyser of flaming oil. Fire raced along the pine-plank floor and up the walls, smeared with pitch to keep out the weather. In its light, the barber rolled, came up onto his knees, and from the shelf beneath the porcelain washbasin snatched up the big Dragoon Colt's pistol he had purchased in St. Louis to defend himself during the trek to Colorado. The man in the doorway was struggling to reload his shotgun when three slugs from the Dragoon struck him in the chest and abdomen. He toppled backward.

A crowd gathered to help put out the fire. Afterward a lantern was brought and someone identified the dead man sprawled in the street as Cecil Goss, the judge's estranged son. Cecil had headed up into the mountains in search of his own claim, but rumor had it he'd grown impatient with the labor and taken to robbing other miners of their ore samples. After some discussion it was decided that he'd heard of the old man's death and come down to blacken the family name further by establishing himself as a man of vengeance. His corpse was hauled away without an inquest and dumped into a hole in Strangers' Corner.

The next day, while sweeping up the cinders and broken glass, Alberto received a visit from Tom Black, the county sheriff. Black, a tall drink of whiskey with fierce handlebars and a powder burn on one cheek, explained that he was not there to arrest the barber for killing Cecil Goss, but to offer him a job.

"Town marshal," he said. "It's unofficial, like the town, which means we can dispense with an election. Pay's fifteen a month plus ten cents for every rat and stray dog you shoot inside town. All it takes is a steady hand."

"I have that," replied the barber.

Since there was no jail, Marshal Pacifico conducted city business from the shop.

Citizens soon grew accustomed to having their complaints heard by a small neat Italian seated in a fancy barber's chair, and for a time Alberto was close to contented. Most of his duties involved breaking up disputes before they escalated into gunplay. Often this was easy. The miners and merchants were by and large good-humored, and the spectacle of standing for a lecture in broken English by a man who had pinched their noses and sprinkled them with lavender water was enough to move them to laughter and dispel bad feelings. When the situation had deteriorated too far for mirth, the marshal dispatched a fast runner to Sheriff Black, who then assumed jurisdiction with the help of a sawed-off Stevens ten-gauge.

But it was no work for a professional man. Alberto pined for his calling, feared his skills would atrophy for want of practice, and could not feed and clothe himself and still keep up the payments on his chair on fifteen dollars per month. Short of a pied piper to lure them down from the mountains and in from surrounding camps, he could not shoot enough rats and stray dogs to prevent his creditors from writing threatening letters. Still he resisted the pressure from his former competitors to sell them his shop and equipment. That would be like Tom Black pawning his guns, or the late Judge Goss trading his dignity and reputation for the dirty bits of gold his son had thieved away.

And so, to forget his misery, he turned to drink.

It began in secrecy, with tiny nips from his bottles of hair tonic. He found the heat in his veins and the humming between his ears a welcome distraction from the gnawing ache that greeted him whenever he looked at his rows of unused mugs, his neglected strops and razors, his silver-plated caster turning green with tarnish. However, to drink in the presence of so many sad reminders was shallow succor at best. Soon he became a familiar sight in all nineteen saloons, stubble-bearded and raggedy-maned, dressed as often as not in one of his old white tunics, buttoned unevenly and covered with stains. Some who saw him remarked that it was a good job the town had not issued its new marshal a badge for him to disgrace. He overheard such comments and didn't care.

There was only one occupation that mattered.

He was slumped over the bar at the King Midas, half asleep, when Rat Brennan accused Oscar Johansen behind the bar of taking a dollar for a fifty-cent shot of whiskey and giving back a quarter and a coat button. The bartender called Brennan a blind Mick, in response to which the quick-tempered prospector clawed out his Colt's Thunderer and clapped the muzzle against Johansen's low forehead, cocking the action. Prodded by a concerned bystander, Marshal Pacifico raised himself on one elbow and asked Brennan what he thought he was doing.

"I'm fixing to blow a little generosity through this damn Scandihoovian's square head."

"I think he means it." The bartender stood unmoving, palms flat on the bar, eyes crossed below the pistol.

"Well, go ahead and do it, then. Don't you tinpanners never finish nothing you start?"

"I ain't fooling!" Brennan's voice was shrill.

"I hope not. I didn't wake up out of a nice dream just to call some Irish bluff." He laid his head on his arms and drifted off. He was back on Cleopatra's barge, giving Julius Caesar the imperial cut. Not even the noise of Rat Brennan's pistol rippled the Nile's smooth green surface.

Tom Black shook him violently. Blinking, Alberto turned his head to watch a bartender he didn't know mopping the floor behind the bar. He had a feeling he'd been out some time. "Where's Oscar?"

"At Penman's," said the sheriff.

Winthrop Penman ran the undertaking parlor. He thought it a strange place for a barman to spend his break.

"Where's Rat?"

"I told the boys to lock him in my basement."

The sheriff's basement was where killers and claim-jumpers awaited trial and hanging. Alberto's foot slipped off the brass rail. He caught his balance and crossed himself. "Dio mio."

"I guess you figured out you ain't marshal no more," Black said. Alberto repeated his invocation.

The sheriff's face was sad. "My fault. I should have knowed you can't take a barber and turn him into no lawman."

"I wish I was a barber," said Alberto.

He pushed away from the bar and tottered out. Crossing the street, he was almost run over by a dray, but kept his course, forcing the cursing driver to steer his team around the man wobbling through the mud. He mounted the boardwalk on the other side and fumbled for his key, then noticed the door to his shop was open. The interior looked bigger. There was a dark rectangle on the floor where the Union Metallic Chair had stood.

He went over and stood in the middle of the rectangle. From there he could see a square of crisp paper on the edge of the basin. He bent over it. The Certificate of Intention to Reclaim Possession was signed by Herbert Spink, Vice President, Accounts Receivable, the Champion Barber Supply Co. of San Francisco.

The Dragoon Colt's he had used to defend himself against Cecil Goss was on its shelf under the basin. He picked it up and left the shop with the big pistol dangling at the end of his arm like a bucket. He turned right and walked until he ran out of board-walk, then stepped down and walked until he ran out of street. He was on the rutted path that led up into the mountains, the route the miners took into town with their ore samples and lists of supplies. The wet earth sucked at his ankles. The rains had ended, but there would be another month of mud before the sun came out and baked everything to the hardness of barber's porcelain.

When he was up to his knees he decided he was too tired to walk any farther. His back was to the mountains. It was a shame he couldn't see them, but he hadn't the energy to turn. He had only enough for one thing.

"Look out, there!"

The shout, and the rattling of the heavy wagon, startled him into turning. He hadn't heard the team plunging down the trail. As he turned, the pistol he had raised turned with him. The driver shouted again. The man seated next to him, who had taken to carrying a shotgun across his lap when Cecil Goss had taken to robbing miners, raised the weapon and tripped both hammers.

When Tom Black got to him he had just enough life left to whisper a request, then sank back into the mud before he could see the sheriff's nod. Because Teamstrike was certain he had died in the act of robbery, Deacon Heppelmeier withheld services and he was buried in Strangers' Corner. But Black kept his word and cabled the profits from the sale of the barbershop and its fixtures to the Pacifico family of Naples; all except twelve dollars for the local stone-cutter, who erected a slab of quality granite at the head of the grave with a simple inscription:

ALBERTO PACIFICO
1840-71
The Best Barber in Teamstrike

THE ALCHEMIST

PART I: THE VISIT OF THE LONG MAN

The long man smelled like a French king.

The scent, heavy with crushed violets and lime water and oil of oleander, was his principal distinguishing feature after his great height, which compelled him to bow his head to clear the lintel and afterward stand with shoulders rounded and his hat off to avoid colliding with the objects that hung from the beams. The hat was a new Stetson, blocked into the Texas pinch, with a brown leather sweatband to which clung a number of cut hairs. He had been to see Juan Morales then, and after his haircut and shave had visited the Aztec Baths and had his brown wool suit brushed and his white shirt boiled in corn water and pressed with a flatiron while he soaked away the hard crust of sweat and sand that had formed like a salt rind during the long ride from the border. His plastered hair was black and glossy, be wore a gringo mustache with ends that trailed, and his thinker's face was long with sorrow. To his vest was pinned a five-pointed star in a shield, nickel-plated, without engraving.

He was perhaps thirty, but his soul was older than even mine.

For a time, as I sat on my tall stool grinding yellow beetles in a mortar, he did not speak or look in my direction, but wandered the dim room, examining with a browser's interest the globes, astrolabes, flaking books, and apothecary jars crowding the plane table and shelves, the stuffed crow perched on the lintel over the doorway, the hard varnished shell of the armadillo suspended by rawhide from the center beam of the ceiling. He squinted at the calligraphy on the labels attached to the jars, trying to make out the foreign words, picked up the skull of a prairie dog, registering surprise that it weighed little more than air, smelled the unfamiliar odors that myself had ceased to smell, of desiccated herbs and she-wolf urine and the exhalations of the athanor. He would know from instinct that these odors were as old as the building itself, permeating the adobe when the clay was yet damp, in the time of the trouble with the Indians up in New Mexico two hundred years ago. Such things cannot be manufactured.

At last he came up to where I sat before the chimney, the table in front of me littered with retorts, iron tongs, wooden scoops, clumps of borax, and my grandfather's bellows, spliced and patched all over so that scarcely a square inch of the original apparatus survived, cleared his throat loudly, and shouted, in dreadful Spanish:

"You are the one the villagers call El Viejo?"

"I am," said I in English, without looking up from my pestle. "It is not necessary to raise your voice. I am not deaf. Merely old."

He blinked, but he dropped his tone. "You speak good American for a Mexican."

"I speak good English for an Englishman. And I am not Mexican. I am Spanish."

"I don't see the difference."

"You would if you came here from Castile with my great-grandfather in fifteen fifty- six."

"Sorry to give offense," he said. "I'm a stranger here. They told me in Socorro you're the man to see when things need fixing that a doctor can't fix. I expected you'd be Indian."

His accent was not Southwestern, nor was it the high honking bray of the Yankee.

He was a Southerner, and he was genuinely apologetic; this too cannot be manufactured. I laid aside my chore.

"I am not a shaman," I said, "although I have learned much from their society that has helped me to subsist in this country. You saw my herb garden on your way to my door. Does it impress you that I have succeeded in making things grow on this bare rock where the rain comes once in three years?"

"I know a piece about growing things. I was raised on a plantation."

"For ten years I employed Yaquis to carry soil by the basket up the naked face of the rock. Nothing grew the first five years. During the next four, the plants reached a height of a sixteenth of an inch, then turned white and died. It was then that I sought out a shaman one-third my age and acquired the secret that has allowed me to harvest my own herbs for seventy-three years. I continue to employ a boy to bring water each day, and once each month to carry and spread horse manure and some other substance that he refuses to identify for anyone but another Yaqui. To know some things it is not enough even to be born in a place to generations born there. You must also share blood."

"What do you pay him with?"

"Instruction works two ways."

He nodded as if he understood. "You've lived here better than eighty years?"

"I was born here one hundred and three years ago."

He said nothing, too polite to express disbelief.

"It is no great personal feat to live a long time," I said.

"It is for me."

I saw then that the sorrow in his face came from behind it, and that his eyes were but the surface of a subterranean pool whose depth was impossible to sound. They were the eyes of my grandfather in a painting made by my father from memory at my request upon the one hundred fourteenth anniversary of his own birth. My grandfather was slain in his ninety-eighth year by the Pueblo Indians in Santa Fe. They pierced his eyes with the lancet he used to bleed lizards and poured molten silver from his own athanor into the sockets, then threw him off a cliff. His third wife fled to this place with my father, who was then in swaddles. He was an alchemist, like his father and grandfather, who left Castile to avoid the inquisitors. We have all sought the secret of the Philosopher's Stone. What we have learned from our failures has been of greater value than what most seekers learn from their successes.

I asked the long man what had brought him so many days from Socorro.

"I ain't from Socorro. I was just riding through. I'm sheriff up in Lincoln County."

I had heard of this place, and of its troubles. I said, "I cannot help you to apprehend fugitives from your justice. It is not the kind of knowledge I possess or pursue."

"I ain't looking to find anyone. I'm looking to get rid of something."

"A sickness?"

"Dreams," he said, circling the brim of his hat

through his long fingers. "I want you to stop the dreams."

———

PART 2: THE PHANTASMS OF THE NIGHT

The long man's name was Pat Garrett. After leaving his birthplace in Alabama he had worked as a cowhand, hunted buffalo, and tended bar in Fort Sumner in the Territory of New Mexico, where he became friendly with a young man named Billy Bonney. Bonney was small-boned and garrulous and spoke incessantly of his plans to take up ranching with a friend named Charlie Bowdre in the Staked Plains of Texas, for which enterprise they were energetically rounding up stray cattle from the big ranches in the County of Lincoln. Bonney carried a big Colt pistol and wore a wide-brimmed sombrero with an Irish-green band.

While in Fort Sumner, Bonney shot and killed a drunk named Joe Grant. A rancher named Chisum then endorsed Pat Garrett's candidacy for the post of Lincoln County sheriff with orders to arrest Bonney, but many people believed Chisum's motives had less to do with Grant than with Bonney's cattle stealing. In a December fight at a place called Stinking Springs, Pat Garrett and his posse killed Charlie Bowdre and took Bonney prisoner, but he later escaped, killing two deputies, and his recapture became a condition of Garrett's continued employment as sheriff.

Finally, in July of that year, Pat Garrett put in at Fort Sumner to ask Pete Maxwell, a mutual friend, if he had heard from Bonney. There, crouched in the dark bedroom of Maxwell's adobe house, Garrett observed a slight figure, naked to the waist and carrying a knife, enter from the next room. Maxwell grasped Garrett's thigh, whispering, "That's him!" Whereupon Pat Garrett produced his Colt pistol and fired twice at close range.

All this had taken place a year ago. In the time between, Bonney's fame had spread like black Spanish moss beyond the boundaries of Lincoln County. He was written of as far east as New York City, where newspaper accounts of his youthful exploits (he was said to be but twenty-one at the time of his death) had inspired a number of fabulists to embellish upon them between the bright paper covers of nickel novels. These found their way into the libraries *of* civilized homes on the Hudson River and the saddle pockets of cowboys not much older than Bonney, who mouthed the unfamiliar words by the light of campfires and lanterns from the grasslands of Nebraska, as flat as a scraping stone, to those same fluted canyons into which Bonney had fled in New Mexico to elude Pat Garrett. In death Billy Bonney had acquired both a legend and a *nombre de guerra* that he had not known in life. As Billy the Kid, his name was spoken in places whose very existence he himself had not suspected.

Pat Garrett acquired notoriety in equal measure. The body had scarcely begun to stiffen when he published a narrative bearing the daunting title *The Authentic Life of Billy the Kid: The Noted Desperado of the Southwest, Whose Deeds of Daring and Blood Made his Name a Terror in New Mexico, Arizona, and Northern Mexico*; and there made public the details of his triumph over this force of lawlessness, if not of his former friendship with it. Although the book did not sell well, Garrett's standing as Bonney's killer increased, and when two vacancies appeared on the New Mexico Territorial Council, Garrett announced his candidacy.

It was at about this time that the dreams began.

One night, arriving home weary and stinking of horse from ten days of riding in search of votes, Pat Garrett poured himself a tall whiskey and stretched his long legs toward the fire. His wife had retired hours before, and not having left home on the best of marital terms he was unwilling to wake her. The big, shabby, leather armchair was suited uniquely to his own physical irregularities, the piñon flames in the kiva fireplace were warm and danced mesmerically, and very soon he dozed. A light sleeper by trade as well as natural inclination, he started awake at the creak of a light footstep on the pine floor, or so he was certain at the time, so vivid were the details of the room and what he heard there.

"Apolinaria?" said he, raising his chin from his chest; for he thought that his wife had entered the room.

"Well, Big Casino," came a voice in response.

Pat Garrett was on his feet in an instant, clawing at his belt for a pistol scabbard that hung there no longer. Only one person in this world had ever addressed him by that name, and in his state of exhaustion Pat Garrett had forgotten that person was dead.

"Billy?"

But this time there was no response. The room was filled with shadows, much like another room he remembered in another house, and though they stirred in the crawling light from the hearth they were empty.

He knew then he had dreamed. He did not suffer physical hardship so well in his maturity as he had when he was a young man in *chaparejos,* and the quest for political support in the bunkhouses and barrios of that vast territory had proven every bit as frustrating as the hunt for Billy Bonney, with the tracks less tangible. Dissipation and strong spirits had made fissures in the walls that enclosed the present, allowing a shade from the past to slip through. He undressed and went to bed, sliding carefully between the crisp linen sheets to avoid waking Apolinaria.

"Quién es?"

Now he sat up rifle straight, and again reached

for a phantom weapon. An exclamation escaped him, startling his wife awake, her hair in her eyes.

And for an instant he saw.

Saw a pale, half-naked figure, translucent in the moonlight shining through the window upon the whitewashed wall facing the bed, approaching in leather breeches only; saw the hairless cylinder of his torso and the slack jaw beneath the band of shadow covering the top half of his face; saw the prominent front teeth, as large as dove's eggs, in the mouth that opened to repeat the question:

"*Quién es?*" Who is it?

Saw the blade in the intruder's hand, shining like cold fire....

And then the figure was gone, evaporated in midstride as completely as the stain of breath upon glass.

Pat Garrett did not tell his wife about the apparition. He explained merely that he had been awakened by a nightmare whose details he could not remember. Apolinaria was Mexican and superstitious. If he told her he had seen Billy Bonney she would insist upon bringing the local padre to the house to make the sign of the cross and pronounce three long and tiresome exorcisms, and Garrett could not abide this particular padre, who considered him an infidel. He turned over, but he did not sleep for hours. Bonney had looked exactly as he had that night in Port Sumner, and asked the very question he had had upon his lips when he died. The scene had not been so real even when Garrett had set it down for publication.

Since then, Pat Garrett had dreamed of Billy dozens of times: at home, in the gaudy and flyblown hotel rooms along the electioneering circuit, lying on the ground beside a fire, sitting upright in a day coach on the A. T. & S. F.; wherever bone-weariness overcame his fear of the phantasms of the night. Sometimes his tormentor was fully dressed in the Spanish costumes he favored, complete with the sombrero with the green band; more often he appeared as he had died, fresh from bed and holding the knife with which he intended to carve himself a piece of beef from Pete Maxwell's storeroom, unaware that soon he would be as cold as the beef. On occasion he recognized Garrett, addressing him as Big Casino. Other times he did not know him. Pat Garrett could not say which Bonney he found more frightening, the swaggering dandy or the sleep fuddled lamb trotting all unknowing to slaughter. He only knew that if the dreams continued he would soon be as mad as those excursionists from Rhode Island who struck out across *La Journada del Muerra* with heads uncovered, jet their brain', frying in the sun like tortillas.

———

PART 3: THE NOSTRUM

I listened without interruption to the narrative of the long man. He was a man on the cusp: when his account touched upon his public life, he spoke in elongated, windy phrases, invoking politicians' fustian; only when it became personal did he subside into the broken, shambling speech of the plantation youth, the western drifter, the laconic lawman. At these times I rather liked him. Insofar as a man of my cloth could ever enjoy the person of an Anglo-Saxon.

"No other words pass between you?" I asked when he fell silent.

He shook his head. "Just them. He calls to me, or he wants to know who I am. That's it."

"I don't suppose you've tried talking back."

"No. Maybe I'm loco, but I ain't so loco as to try talking to a dead man."

"And yet who among us possesses the wisdom of the dead?" I stepped down from the stool and crossed the room conscious that with each step I eradicated a measure of whatever belief he held that I had passed the century mark; for it was only since my ninetieth year that I paid heed to the fine two rungs on the ladder that led from my rock to the desert floor. From a high shelf I brought down an apothecary jar, removed its glass lid to sniff at its contents, and replaced the lid.

"Do you know grams?" said I.

"I sure don't."

"A teaspoon will suffice, or a quarter of a jigger if you haven't a spoon. Heat that amount over a low flame until it liquefies, then swallow it, just before retiring. The dreams should stop."

He peered at the label. "That Mexican?"

"Latin. You wouldn't understand it even if you could translate *it*. My people have used it as a nostrum against phantasms since before Christ."

"It smells it." He wrinkled his nose and clamped down the lid.

"Come back if the dreams continue."

"Ain't you got any more faith in your medicine than that?"

"One day it will be gone. The same is not always true of a ghost's patience."

"I don't believe in ghosts any more than I believe in God or the Devil," he said. "Perhaps if you live to be as old as I you will not be so certain about the Devil."

"How much?" He produced a drawstring pouch from the pocket of his trousers.

"I have no need of money. The villagers provide me with food and I have no reason to leave my rock."

"What, then?"

"Bring me wisdom."

He bounced the pouch on his palm. The coins shifted and clanked. He smiled then, as slowly as shadows lengthening. "That's a stiff bargain, seeing as I got so little to spare."

"It is the only medium of exchange I honor."

"Just what kind of wisdom are you wanting?"

"You will recognize it," I said. "When the dreams stop."

He put away the pouch and tugged on his big hat. At the door he stopped and looked back. The long solemn face clouded with thought. "I'm kind of a long time paying my debts. It's a failing."

"I will be here. I am always here."

He left my shop. He remained in my thoughts.

The nostrum is but a sleeping draught, distilled of poppies and wormwood, with oil of creosote to bind. It was first corn-posed by my great-great-grand-father, alchemical master to King Philip II, to send that ruler to the black depths below the level where dwelled the demons that gnawed at him in the dark. In return, my clever ancestor was granted the whole of Chihuahua, of which the rock upon which stands my simple workshop is all that remains. My great-great-grandfather was a quack, a mere puffer who worked his bellows to no good purpose but his own exalted station. He was drawn and quartered when his crystal failed to reveal the Armada's destruction. But his nostrum has its uses.

————

PART 4: THE RETURN OF THE LONG MAN

These things I heard; for a lone village in a naked desert draws travelers as spring water draws the creatures that fly and the beasts that crawl, and wisdom is the coin of my tiny realm.

Membership in the New Mexico Territorial Council did not come to Pat Garrett. He lost in a close election after he accosted the author of a spurious letter to the Rio Grande Republican on the subject of his character and battered him about the head with the Colt he had used to kill Billy Bonney. (Whether this incident cost him votes or attracted them was a matter of lively discussion in certain quarters.) Disenchanted with public life, he retired to his thousand-acre ranch on the Rio Hondo, but that existence only made him restless, and in rapid succession he served as a captain with the Texas Rangers, managed a detective agency in the Panhandle, and formed the Pecos Valley Irrigation Company, tapping the liquid wealth of the artesian springs that lay beneath Roswell, New Mexico. When that palled, he ran for sheriff of Chavez County, but lost, then accepted a governor-appointed post as sheriff in Doña Ana County. He was by every account a hard man behind a star, short in his dealings with citizens and brutal with prisoners; a driven man, many said, running roughshod over his office as if something were flogging him from deep inside.

I thought that it would not be long before the long man returned to my door.

In this I was wrong. The years passed, slowly in the desert, like gilas on their pale bellies, and for many of them I heard nothing of Pat Garrett.

Villagers and strangers came to me with their complaints, shouting them at the top of their lungs as my eardrums thickened. I slept at a level close to waking, I shrank in stature, my joints swelled and pained me when the monsoons came. But my eyes were keen, and my mind was as a thing honed by the wisdom that came my way in small quantities, like grit on a grindstone. I felt an urgency to unlock the key to the transmutation of base metal, an urgency unique in my long line. I had no grandchildren, no children. The thick and braided vine with roots in the court of Carolus Magnus ended with me. There would be none to work the bellows when I relinquished the handles; no hand would take up my pestle when I set it down at last. I who now had lived in three centuries would close a way of life that was already ancient when the Pyramids of Egypt rose from the quarries.

Clay to iron, iron to steel. The son of the boy who carried water to my garden when first the long man came, a father now himself, assisted me when I could not apprentice myself, recording the long list of failures in the yellow leaves of my notebook when I was unable to hold a pen and gathering the coals to feed the athanor when my back would not bend. Tin to bronze, bronze to brass. The books I had read rotted on the shelves, like oranges that had surrendered their juices and whose seeds were barren.

Quicksilver to silver; elusive. Silver to gold; unlikely. But if clay to iron and clay to gold, why not iron to gold? Not for personal wealth, never that, but for the benefit of knowledge, and of man's mastery of the natural world. Iron to rust, rust to clay. Gold to gold. Gold did not oxidize; of all the metals it was the only one to break the circle. There was the lock that fit the key.

In a seizure of pique I threw my grains of ore into the fire. They ignited, sending sparks up the flue.

"Well, you ain't no ghost, that's a fact. You told me once't there's no end to a ghost's patience."

I started; for age and command had brought an edge to the long man's tone that overcame my deafness.I turned my head. Gaunt he was now, his hair and mustache white, and the years of stooping to hear and to be heard had rounded his back. The long face was as brown and cracked as a dry lake-bed. His suit of clothes was smarter than the one he had worn on his first visit, and now that the railroads had come it had no need of brushing. He no longer smelled like a French king, but like harnesses that had been left in the weather. Where the nickel-plated star had been depended a platinum chain with a staghorn fob. The hat in his hand was a slouch with a four-inch brim and a wide silk band. The sorrow he wore was the same.

"The nostrum has run out," said I.

"Years and years ago. It never did stop even one dream."

"Did you follow the instructions I gave you?"

"A quarter of a jigger a night for two years. After

that I switched to whiskey. That didn't stop them neither, though it did sunny up my disposition. We had us some fine talks, Billy and me."

After a time, so Pat Garrett told it, the half-naked Bonney of Fort Sumner came less often. Mostly it was Billy in his Spanish costume and green-banded sombrero, although sometimes he appeared in the same caved-in black hat and heavy cable sweater he had posed in for the photograph that still circulated on cigarette cards throughout the Southwestern United States. He spoke of old times with Chisum and John Tunstall, the English rancher for whom Bonney once worked, and whose death in the Lincoln County range war had triggered the events that led eventually to that bedroom crawling with shadows in Fort Sumner. He spoke of dealing monte in Garrett's saloon. On occasion he brought cards, and the pair played poker until dawn, or until Pat Garrett awoke. Often the visits were quite ordinary. The thing Garrett dreaded—and because he could not predict when it would happen even the ordinary visits were torturous—was the times when Bonney's amiable, slack-jawed expression would change suddenly in the middle of some folksy anecdote or while he was drawing from the deck; when his skin would grow ashen and a black band of shadow would fall across the top half of his visage, and he would shout: "*Quién es?*" Then there would be an explosion, very loud, well beyond the volume entrusted to a mere dream, and Garrett would wake up, bathed in icy sweat, his nostrils burning with the stench of sulfur and cordite. It required half of a bottle of whiskey to help him back to sleep; whereupon another dream would come, or it would not. When it came there was no determining whether it would play itself out peacefully or end in the same disturbing way.

He did not always dream. When he did not, and when the dreams were peaceful, his life the next day would go one way or the other, as do all our days. In time, however, he came to see that the death-dream, in which he killed his friend, invariably preceded a black day in his passage. He had slain Billy Bonney the night before he pistol-whipped the writer of the letter to *the Rio Grande Republican,* and subsequently lost the Territorial Council election. He was defeated for sheriff in Chavez County on a day following a night during which he had slain Billy Bonney. He had not dreamed at all before making the acquaintance of President Theodore Roosevelt, who appointed Pat Garrett a collector of customs at El Paso. During Roosevelt's second term, Garrett one night revealed in ghastly detail the circumstances of Bonney's death; the next day he allowed the president to be photographed with himself and a notorious saloon-keeper, and when the matter was brought to the abstemious Roosevelt's attention, Pat Garrett lost his appointment. There were other such episodes, but the above serves to establish the pattern.

"Is it your belief that Bonney is responsible for

all your misfortunes?" I asked. "Not all. No man's lucky all the time. But the ones I brung up suit Billy's damn sense of humor down to the ground. Take that time he kilt Olinger and Bell and jumped jail. He done it to vex me as much as to keep from getting hung."

"Ghosts enjoy a joke as well as the next man."

He made no response, but shifted his weight on his big mirrored boots. I turned up a palm. "What is it you ask of me?"

"I come down here thinking you'd have some nostrum that works where the other didn't. It's been better than twenty-five years. I reckon that makes you a hunnert and twenty-eight."

"Twenty-nine; I was born on Twelfth Night. The one I gave you was three hundred years old. There have been no developments."

"That tears it then. Last time I kilt Billy I got into a fight next day with one of my tenant ranchers over some goats he ran on my property. I can't abide a goat. I'm meeting him tomorrow to iron it all out, but I wanted to make sure I didn't dream about killing Billy tonight."

"I am sorry."

He tugged on his slouch hat with the same gesture he had used a quarter-century before. Perhaps it was this similarity that brought to his mind our words of parting on that occasion. The same gradual grin deepened the cracks in his face.

"I clean forgot to bring any of that wisdom you

asked for," he said. "I told you I'm slow settling debts."

"I am confident that you pay the ones that matter."

The next day—I learned of it many months later, from a New Mexico taxidermist who tried to purchase my armadillo—Pat Garrett argued on the Las Cruces road with a tenant over goats. The long man was shot twice with a Colt pistol while sitting on his buckboard and died before he struck the earth. I do not know if the night before the encounter he dreamed of killing Billy Bonney. All things that come from clay go back to it in the end. Save gold.

IRON HEART'S STORY

Porcupine Woman and Sees Water were concerned about Iron Heart.

"He speaks of nothing but things dead," Sees Water declared. "He is a great hero of our people, but he grows older with each story."

Porcupine Woman, mother to Sees Water and Iron Heart's mate these past forty winters, continued to drag the strip of hide in her hands back and forth across the stone resting in her lap. Those hands now were as coarse as the stone was smooth, worn so from long use, as if the two surfaces had traded places. "It is the way of the People to say these things many times to our young, that they will remember and speak of them to their children, and they to theirs. In this way the deeds of our heroes do not drift away like the dry snow that comes in the Moon of Dead Trees."

"I understand this. Still, my father has lost

interest in everything but the old stories. I think that he is waiting to die."

Porcupine Woman considered. It was a custom of her people, called the Cut Arms by their friends the Sioux, and the Cheyenne by the white long knives such as those who had followed the Yellow Hair chief to attack the People at the Washita the winter before, to listen betimes to the counsel of the young, who saw things differently and sometimes more dearly than their wiser elders. And Sees Water, whose breasts were high and whose face knew no creases, was uncommonly grave and thoughtful for one of her small years.

"Iron Heart is a great warrior," Porcupine Woman said. "He has stolen many horses from our enemies the Crow and counted many coup, and so has earned the right to speak of these things. It is just as true that he remembers the color of the feathers in the headdress of Spotted Calf, dead these twenty summers, at the cost of forgetting whether he broke his own fast this morning. This is bad, for he is not as old as old Broken Lodge, who has seen seventy winters and rides and shoots as well as a brave half his age. Yet he seems older."

"What shall we do, Mother?"

"In old times I would suggest that he go to the buffalo, or steal horses from the Crow. But the buffalo grow smaller in number each winter, and we have given our word to the great white chief of the long knives that we will live in peace with the Crow if they will do the same with us."

"Then he will die surely. The Wise One Above does not grant the gift of life to those who are not thankful."

During Porcupine Woman's silence the sun moved. The hide grew softer with each motion across the stone. At length she spoke.

"Be of good heart, child. Your mother is old, but she has not forgotten those things that set a man's heart afire. We shall go to Iron Heart and ask him to tell us one of the old stories."

The face of Sees Water fell. "Mother, you have not heard me. It is the old stories that are killing him."

"This one will save him."

They went to Iron Heart, who sat cross-legged in a patch of suit holding up a tooth that had fallen from his head, staring at it as if it contained some great truth. His long hair had gone as gray as his name and the skin had begun to hang from his bones, but in the old face Porcupine Woman always saw the handsome brave who had taken her to his lodge when her summers were but sixteen. They sat facing him.

"The Powder River will freeze this winter," said he without greeting. "The beaver plew will be as thick as the grass that comes after the planting rain."

Porcupine Woman said, "The beaver are gone, my husband. The last one left before Sees Water first saw the sun."

"Sam Tyree said he will trade two bolts of

gingham for each good plew." The women exchanged glances.

"Sam Tyrce was killed by the Pawnee the year the snow forgot to fall," Porcupine Woman said.

"I think I shall ask for three bolts. Sam Tyree will cheat us if we let him."

"Speak not of him. Tell us of the time you and I and Mounts-His-Horse-Funny tried to skin the grandfather elk."

Iron Heart turned the tooth between his fingers. "Why must I speak of this thing? You were there."

"No one tells it as well as you, and Sees Water wishes to hear it." She prodded her daughter with her elbow.

"Yes, Father," said Sees Water, with a start. "Tell of the time you and Mother and Mounts-His-Horse-Funny tried to skin the grandfather elk."

"It is a long story. My belly is empty."

"Your bowl is still warm from your last meal, my husband. Tell the story."

He filled and emptied his lungs with great resignation. But his eyes glittered. He deposited the tooth in the medicine bag tied around his neck, forgetting in his eagerness that the tooth was his own and as such carried no medicine for him.

"It was in the Summer That Should Have Been Autumn," he said. "Mounts-His- Horse-Funny and I had been in the high country for eight suns, shooting birds and rabbits and looking for larger game to feed the camp."

Porcupine Woman touched his knee. "My husband, the Summer That Should Have Been Autumn was not the time. It was in the Spring That Stayed Dead, when the snow refused to melt."

"It was the hot autumn. Old Standing Hawk fell dead of the heat."

"No, you are thinking of the time his wife gave birth to a dead son. Standing Hawk died the next autumn."

After a moment he nodded. "You are right. The hunt was the first time I wore the robe you made from the white buffalo. The air was cold."

"Tell the story, my husband."

"I am telling it. The camp was starving because of the cold. The buffalo did not come that time and we were heading for the mountains to look for the long-legged kind. Porcupine Woman came along to hold the horses when we climbed. You were not born yet, Daughter."

"It was her first spring," Porcupine Woman corrected. "I left her with White Water Woman, the sister of your mother."

His glitter faded. "What is that to the story?"

"You have always spoken of the importance of telling these tales the same way every time if they are to be remembered as they happened."

"This is so." Nodding absently, he looked far off, past the broken peaks of the tall rocks the white long knives called the Tetons; for there, in the silvery mists beyond the edge of the world, resided the people and things he found and brought back for his listeners. With each winter he saw them more clearly than those he walked among on this side. The day would come, he knew, when he would decide to stay with them rather than return to this place of fading shadows.

"Mounts-His-Horse-Funny had a blue roan which he stole from a Crow chief. Only Mounts could ride it, for it stamped its forefeet and showed its teeth to anyone else who approached. It pulled up lame and Mounts got off to see what was the matter."

"It was a pinto, and everyone could ride it who wished to except Mounts, whom it threw off at every opportunity. That was why he was afoot to see the grandfather elk."

Sees Water glanced annoyedly at her mother, who seemed determined not to let Iron Heart continue the story which she said would pull him back from the land of mists. But Porcupine Woman had eyes only for her husband.

"It was a roan. Mounts traded it to Standing Hawk for his daughter Crab Woman and a breast-plate made from the bones of one hundred and forty field mice. Hawk gave it back when he found he could not ride it."

"You are thinking of Black Bull. Mounts was married to Wool Woman, who came to him after the death of her husband Runs-in-the-Rain."

"I remember this unimportant thing. Mounts fell off the pinto and tore his legging. When he bent to look at it, he saw the elk track at his feet. He thought it was buffalo and we began to follow it. Two suns and two sleeps we followed, high into the mountain where the air is hard to breathe. By then we had seen its droppings and knew they were those of the buffalo, though its hoofprint was larger than any elk's known to us, or to our fathers, or to their fathers. A spread hand would not cover it.

"The third sun was barely clear of the earth when we broke camp and saw it against the sky. We thought at first it was a trick of the mist, which fools the eye and makes a thing seem larger than it is. Bigger than any buffalo it was, the points upon its antlers as many as the wild ponies that ran in the land before the first long knives came. Its hide was as red as blood."

"Brown," Porcupine Woman said. "Brown like hickory, and it was not so big as that, though it weighed as much as a buffalo cow."

Iron Heart's glare was black. "Does my wife prefer this story to come from her lips?"

"No one tells it as well as you, my husband."

"It is so. I was carrying the musket that cost me twelve plew and a blanket at Bent's Fort, and I fired at the same time Mounts released a shaft from his bow. I do not know even now which of us delivered the fatal injury. The elk ran the length of a lance thrust and fell. We removed the entrails and fashioned a travois from the boughs of the lodgepole pine to drag the carcass back to camp, for neither of our horses would bear its weight. Then came the difficult business of removing the hide.

"No knife would penetrate its thick skin," he continued. "No axe would part its fibers. I myself broke a clovis point fashioned by my great-grandfather in the time of the white king, trying to make the first notch. We had first to place the tools in a fire until they glowed as red as the lifting sun that they would burn through the hide and hair. Still it would not surrender its hold upon the flesh. At last we hitched both our horses to the burned edge and slapped their rumps, that they would bolt and tear it away from the carcass. The turtle that carries the sun upon its back crossed the sky in the time it took to skin the grandfather elk."

Porcupine Woman cleared her throat. The face Iron Heart turned upon her was a stone slab. Yet he said nothing, allowing her to speak.

"It was not a clovis point you broke, but a bone knife. You always did insist upon using a fleshing tool for cutting. And we hitched one horse to the hide, not two. The turtle that carries the sun had half its journey still ahead of it when we traded six plew, not twelve, for the musket you bought at Bent's Fort. Even then you were cheated. It misfired that day, and so it was Mounts-His-Horse-Funny's arrow that killed the elk, which fell where it stood and did not run. But for those small things you told the story perfectly."

"Bah!" He scrambled to his feet and strode in the

direction of the horses. "Where are you going, my husband?"

"To the tall rocks, who will listen to my stories without interruption." Moments later the women heard the rataplan of hoofs fading from camp.

"I have not seen Father so angry in many moons," Sees Water declared. "Why did you upset him so?"

Rising, Porcupine Woman shook the dust from the hem of her doeskin. "The story of the time we skinned the grandfather elk is one of the few he never tells right. Whenever I correct him, the blood comes into his face and the fire into his eyes and he is as he was the day I gave him my heart. He will be like this for a long while."

"And when he is over it?"

"Then I shall ask him to tell us of the time he and Otter Belt swam across the Canadian to steal horses from the Kiowa. He never tells that one right either." She touched one of her daughter's braids. "Come, child. Your father will bring back game to prepare and we must have our work done."

THE DEATH OF DUTCH CREEL

When they went and made a moving picture about Dutch, I swore I'd never go see it. They didn't ask me to help, for one thing, and the only way I found out they done it at all, I read it was coming to the old Ladybird Theater in Absaroka. But saying you'll do or not do a thing is easier to make good on when you're not married, and still twice as easy when you're married to anyone but Addie.

She got on me about how was I to know it was no good if I didn't go look at it, and how even if it was no good, it still beat sitting home night after night the way we usually done, and how she never took no vow to spend all her evenings sewing samplers and reading *The Oklahoma Farmer*, and all, and finally just to shut her up I took her in the flivver to the Ladybird and we went and seen it. These moving pictures are the end of married peace.

It was some show. This curly-headed fellow that was made out to be Dutch Creel wore a tall black hat and two guns low and used them both at the same time, never just the one and then border-shifting when it run out of cartridges, which was the way they done it in the wild days. He stuck up banks and stagecoaches and jumped on trains and swapped lead with the laws and occasionally dropped one, and there was so much dust and smoke you swore you heard gunshots and hoofbeats, though of course there wasn't no sound, just this skinny tenderheel banging a piano up by the screen like he was slapping hornets.

Addie, she loved it. She had fried a chicken and packed it in a wicker basket, and every time one of them bullets went home, she bit into a leg or a wing till there wasn't nothing left but the bones, and I begun to worry if she'd leave even them for the hogs. I never got none of it.

After twenty minutes or so, the laws cornered old Dutch in a shack in a box canyon and this big good-looking jasper that was supposed to be Sheriff Rube Belford went in alone and outdrawed him and that there was the end. It was some show all right.

Everybody that was in that theater that night went home happy as a bitch dog.

Everybody but me.

It didn't none of it happen that way, you see; especially the last part. I'm fixing to put the whole kit down here just as it was, and I will swear on a wagonload of King James Bibles it's the goods. I was there.

Kind of.

You already know about the guns. They come dear in them days. If you had a pistol at all—shotguns and squirrel rifles was like hoes to a granger and common as outhouses—well, you was right royal. Two pistols was gilding the lily, and if you still had the wherewithal to buy cartridges for to practice with and get good with both hands, I don't know why you'd feel the need to stick up even one bank. Which was as many as Dutch ever stuck up before deciding while he was healing, that bank-robbing weren't his specialty. Stopping trains wasn't, neither; and since even then stagecoaches was as scarce as river ferries are now, they was plenty safe from him too. Dutch stole livestock.

Not that he was your everyday horse thief or rustler, riding off on another man's transportation while the man was indoors bellying up to some fancy. Dutch and his gang could slip an entire herd out from under the nighthawks' noses slick as spit outside El Paso on Wednesday and sell it to some fat Spanish grandee in Chihuahua on Friday, then run that same grandee's remuda across the river on their way back north and sell it on Sunday to the cattleman whose beef they stole in the first place. Done it, too, on more than one occasion, and likely still would be, if not for that thing in El Paso in '99. But that's taking a daily before the lariat is throwed, and I'll come to it.

The curly hair was wrong too. Dutch was Cherokee on his ma's side and his hair hung straight as a stovepipe and just as black. He was born in the Nations, what's called Oklahoma now, where the Five Civilized Tribes lived under the protection of Judge Parker's court in Fort Smith, over the border in Arkansas. Leastwise they did when bad white men wanted for crimes in other places wasn't hiding out there, stirring up six kinds of hell and bringing the laws in after them. Ford Harper, he was one.

Ford was around twenty when he come, nobody knew where from, though most said Missouri, and lost no time taking up with a Creek widow near twice his age, baptized Mary Elizabeth Treefall, whose first husband had left her a section over by McAlester. White men was not let own property in the Nations unless they was married to Indians.

In the spring of '96, Ford hired Dutch, who was then eighteen, to help him work the spread, which Ford had took it in his head was tailormade for raising horses. Well, Dutch and Ford got on right handy, being so close in age and temperament, and with them two out mending fence all day and cutting the wolf loose in McAlester nights don't reckon poor old Mary Treefall seen much of her new man after Dutch come on. I don't know if she found that satisfactory, but she hadn't no complaints to make about the way the ranch was run, because inside of six months they had twice as many horses as they started with.

One night, five of Parker's marshals and two trackers rode onto the Treefall spread when everyone was in bed and called upon Ford to surrender himself for the crime of rustling in the Nations. They had the house surrounded and enough weapons between them to take Canada away from Queen Victoria. But Canada didn't have Dutch Creel.

He slept up in the hayloft of the barn with a new Model 1894 Winchester he bought on his rustler's wages. When the bellering woke him up, he crawled over to the opening and drew a bead on one of the riders and plucked him clean out of his saddle. It was a lucky shot by moonlight, but it made him his reputation from then on as a gunman and someone to walk around. The fact that he never duplicated it is a matter of no consequence to the legend.

Right away those marshals changed their minds about the house and opened up on the barn. Dutch shot back and they returned fire, and pretty soon that barn had enough holes in it to stand for a corncrib, though the only casualty turned out to be a plug mare in a stall on the ground that picked up a slug in its right haunch and a predisposition against lawmen for the rest of its days. They wasn't much better marksmen than Dutch, you see.

But the odds were poor and Dutch knowed it. When the marshals set fire to a hay wagon and started it toward the barn to burn him out, he dumb down and surrendered. Ford Harper meanwhile had shinnied down the rainpipe from the upstairs bedroom he shared with Mary Treefall and lit out.

The laws took Dutch in irons to Fort Smith, where as it turned out he had been lucky in his choice of targets, as the man he shot was not a marshal but a Choctaw tracker and hit only in the leg, though he did finally have to have it cut off. When the jury handed in the guilty verdict, Parker put the lie to that Hanging Judge tag the Eastern papers hung on him and sentenced Dutch to fourteen years in the Detroit House of Corrections.

Accounts vary on just how the prisoner busted loose of his armed escort on the way to the train station. Some say Ford went and got up a gang and shot him out. The Fort Smith paper said Dutch overpowered a marshal still under the influence from a birthday celebration the night before and got his pistol. More than likely, Ford paid someone in the escort to slip Dutch a weapon; some of them marshals wasn't no better than bandits theirselves, and Ford always was the kind to let his poke do his talking for him, it being the one thing he had managed to rescue along with his hide when he left the lreettili spread in such a hurry. However it happened, Dutch got away in a hail of lead that didn't hit much of anyone or anything, and Ford Harper was seen driving the buckboard he was riding in.

I reckon that's where the legend got its start. Rustlers in those parts was thicker than mosquito wigglers, but desperadoes that bucked Judge Parker's justice come few and far between. It didn't hurt, neither, that a New York journalist happened to be in Fort Smith to interview the Judge at the time of the escape and wrote a nickel novel called The Border Bandit, or For the Love of a Creek Princess, in which he lopped twenty years off Mary Treefall's true age and transferred her affections from Ford to Dutch.

There would be a dozen more before Dutch was through, with not enough truth in the whole batch of them to sink a cement boat.

Meanwhile Dutch and Ford was on the run with a hundred dollars reward on each of their heads. They stopped at the ranch for horses and rode down to Texas, where Ford had a married sister raising cattle and tumbleweeds on a little spread north of Dallas. They made theirselves useful there and might have had permanent positions in the cow trade if Ford's brother-in-law that owned the spread hadn't lost it one night in a poker game in Dallas and then got himself killed when he tried to draw a hideout gun on the winner.

Dutch and Ford had a falling-out then. Ford wanted to go down to Old Mexico, but Dutch was all for heading back to the Nations and taking up where they left off, wanted men or no. So they split up. Ford's sister Henrietta went with Dutch.

A word about Henrietta. She was a tough little redhead brought up by a widowed father in a family of boys and had been doing a man's work since she was ten. She was pretty, too, with a direct way of speaking that appealed to a man of Dutch's temperament. I'm not saying they done anything before Henrietta's husband drawed to an inside straight and a bellyful of lead, but they become right friendly after the fact.

With a woman to support, Dutch got right to work doing the thing he done best. He put her up with Mary Treefall, who had been running the horse ranch alone in Ford's absence, and got together a gang in McAlester. His reputation was well along by then and finding recruits wasn't the problem it might have been a year or so earlier. Two of them, Bob Stonemason and Dick Leaping Deer, deserve mention here because they went on to greater fame with their own outfits after Dutch's death.

It was with this bunch that Dutch got most of his glory. When they was about, there wasn't a string of horses or a herd of cattle safe between Little Rock and Chihuahua.

The law looked hard, but the law didn't have many friends in the Nations. News of posses spread like telegraph. Dutch was always gone from the ranch when they come to call, and Mary and Henrietta always swore they hadn't seen him in weeks. The reward for his capture went up to a thousand dollars.

When you're that good at what you do, the thing you most got to watch out for is yourself. Dutch didn't. He got to believing what the papers said about him, how he had a second sight that made him invincible, and he got to thinking how a gift like his was wasted on livestock. He had his heart set on robbing a bank.

The one he chose was the Cattleman's Trust in El Paso. He'd read about it in the *Police Gazette,* which reported the bank's assets at a million and a half dollars and announced that its security was the best in the West, with a newfangled time lock on the vault and six armed Pinkerton guards on duty around the clock. It seemed a proper challenge for the Bandit of the Border.

I personally think Dutch's decision not to ever rob another bank had less to do with how the raid come off than the amount of time he put into planning it. That was work, which if he'd been willing to do in the first place he wouldn't have took up the outlaw trail. It was a good plan that had a lot to do with timing. It might even have been a great plan, but we'll never know, because the law in El Paso got wind of it somehow and was waiting for the gang when they rode up.

It wasn't no day for plans. The one the law thought up was to let Dutch and the rest get inside the bank and then open fire on them when they come out with the cash, but one of the amateurs in the posse didn't think much of that plan and started the ball by shooting the hat off Dick Leaping Deer's head as he was dismounting in front of the hitching rail.

At that point the fighting became general. The laws poured lead into the gang of horsemen and the outlaws fired back from the porch and from behind the cover of watering troughs and their own mounts. Two of Dutch's men, Harvey Narr and Alkali Ed McGrath, was killed outright, and a third, Sam Cutnose, died of his wounds the next day in the city jail. The law lost four men and a Swede named Lindstrom got his head blowed clean off by a shotgun when he come running around the corner to see what all the noise was about. They laid that to the Creel gang, but Bob Stonemason maintained until the day they hung him that nobody in Dutch's outfit was carrying a scattergurk that day.

The laws, figuring they had a sure thing, hadn't bothered to close off the street, and in all the smoke and shouting, Dutch and Bob managed to get mounted and took off in two directions. Dick got his horse shot out from under him when he had one foot in the stirrup and Dutch, seeing his predicament, wheeled around and galloped back through all that hell and pulled him up behind his own saddle. He was shot twice for his trouble, once in the left thigh and once through the right lung.

The posse caught up with Bob, himself suffering with a slug in his back, north of El Paso, where he'd ridden under the notion that he was heading south toward the Mexican border, and arrested him without a fight. They dug the slug out of him and patched him up and sent him to the Huntsville penitentiary for life. Two years later he escaped, assembled a bunch of his own, and raised six kinds of hell throughout Texas until the Rangers pulled him out of a whorehouse in Austin and put a rope around his neck.

Dick Leaping Deer doctored Dutch's wounds as best he could and took him to a nothing ranch outside Juarez. It took an Indian to find the place, following directions provided by Dutch during his semi-lucid periods. Now, the last thing Ford Harper expected, having taken up with a woman named Juanita Flores on a tenant basis in the northwest corner of a spread the size of California, was to have his past come smack to his doorstep this way. But being Ford and therefore soft on his old compadres, he took them both in, and between him and Dick and Juanita they brung Dutch through a bad patch of pneumonia back to health. After a few weeks, in answer to a coded telegram sent to a trusted friend in McAlester, Henrietta come all the way from the Nations to help with the nursing.

She also brung news that I like to think helped the healing process along: She was expecting Dutch's child.

By and by, frisky with the knowledge that he was going to be a pa, Dutch made plans to go back home. Mary Treefall had sent word with Henrietta that the outlaw life was no life for a family man and that she wouldn't mind taking Dutch on as a partner in the horse-raising business, provided he held the stolen stock down to a respectable minimum. The lesson he had had in the matter of his invincibility had not been lost on him during his long convalescence. He was all fired up to give the straight life a whirl.

Dick and Henrietta wasn't so sure. For one thing, the reward for his capture since El Paso now came to twenty-five hundred dollars dead or alive, which made him a more valuable property than ever to certain of his friends and neighbors, most of whom didn't have a penny to pitch or a place to pitch it. For another, he was in no condition to travel. Dick had been able to pry the slug out of Dutch's thigh on the way from Texas, but nobody knew nothing about removing the one that had passed through his lung, so it was still inside him. Also, he was just over the pneumonia, a tricky complaint that has a sidewindy habit of bending back around and biting you just when you think it's had enough. They asked him to wait another month.

Dutch wouldn't listen, no sir. What he wanted was home. So the three of them said goodbye to Ford and Juanita and left in the buckboard Henrietta had come in on.

It wasn't no trip for a man without his strength. They had to keep to the back roads to avoid Rangers, and that made it near twice as long, especially it being December and pumphandle cold. Pretty soon Dutch took with fever. He was out of his head when they put into Nacogdoches and rented a bed in a rooming house for Dutch and

Henrietta while Dick fetched a doctor. The landlady she recognized the sick man from a wanted
dodger and soaked them for most of the cash they
had, on account of the risk. That didn't leave them
but just enough to pay the doctor, who listened to
Dutch's chest and pried back his eyelids and told
them they oughtn't to be wasting a medical man's
time when any fool could see what they needed was
a priest.

Dutch Creel fooled him, though. He lived into
the next day and past sundown that evening, with
Henrietta not budging from his side the whole time
except to find water for to bathe his forehead when
he was burning up and an extra blanket to cover him
with when his teeth chattered. It was all just marking
time. Dick, he poked his head in finally to see if she
needed anything and found her sitting next to the
bed holding Dutch's hand, and he knowed by the
stillness in the room that there was a dead man in it.
It was Christmas Eve, 1899.

A quiet passing, you say, for such an unquiet
soul. But the story ain't finished, not by a long shot.
Because right then was when Henrietta told Dick
Leaping Deer about Dutch's last request.

It seemed that he had come out of his fog just
long enough to ,make it, then shut his eyes and never
said another word until Henrietta noticed he had
stopped breathing.

Dick, he listened, not sure at first if she was
telling it true or if the tragic situation had unhinged

her. By the end of it he was grinning in spite of his loss.

"Dutch," he said, "you son of a bitch."

Henrietta, who was level-headed for a woman and not one to waste time blubbering when work needed doing, agreed with Dick's assessment of the dead man's character in all its good-natured spirit. She had already made up her mind to do the thing. Dick wanted to help, but being on the run himself was forced to lay low while Henrietta went alone to the sheriff's office.

Now, Rube Belford was a good old boy to be pinned to a star. Twice a widower, he was coming up on sixty and was a deacon in the Presbyterian church who'd run a harness shop in town for twenty years before retiring to the job of peace officer. The moving picture my Addie and me seen made him out tall and rangy and kind of handsome, but he was built more along the lines of a parlor stove and ugly as a mud fence. You'd have to have made his acquaintance for at least five minutes to realize he had a heart as big as his big bald head.

But he was a businessman, and after a little haggling, he agreed to "Miz Creel's" proposition. Before locking up the office to escort her back to the rooming house, he selected a Stephens ten-gauge from among the shotguns and rifles in the rack and loaded it with double-ought buck; I seen the gun once in this little museum in Absaroka before it burned to the ground with everything inside, including an Old

Sharps pistol I donated myself that Dutch used to carry around for potting rattlers with when he mended fence.

The rooming house landlady had retired for the evening. Henrietta let the sheriff in the front door quiet as a preacher's daughter saying good night to a beau and led him to the little hail bedroom where Dutch lay. Dick wasn't nowhere about, but before he left, he had got Dutch into his clothes and propped him up against the headboard of the bed with his Colt in his lap. Rube Belford, he looked over the situation and told Henrietta to take the air. Commands weren't much good with her since she was a tomboy on her daddy's farm, but she didn't want to be around for what the sheriff was fixing to do and so she obeyed. She wasn't gone two minutes when she heard the roar of that big Stephens.

Belford had never before shot a man, but he weren't nobody's fool.

He put nine double-ought slugs into the middle of Dutch's dead body, avoiding the face so no one could claim mistaken identity and cause the ranchers that put up that bounty to keep the twenty-five hundred for theirselves. Just to be sure there was no cheating done, he wired the Pinkerton office in Houston on Christmas morning, and they sent out a man to take pictures of Dutch strapped to a door for Bertillon measurements, which was a scientific process to guard against ringers.

In due course the reward was paid. Sheriff

Belford gave half to Henrietta as agreed, and that money come in right handy when she went back to the Treefall spread and hired a foreman and crew and stock to run. She held a little aside for Dick Leaping Deer, but he never come to collect. You can read in your history texts what he done with a gang of his own in Texas before he went down to South America or someplace and just got swallowed up. A month or so after the papers carried Rube Belford's hair-raising account of his shoot-out with the great desperado, he told it again to a book writer, who published it as *The True and Authentic Life of "Dutch" Creel, By His Slayer*. It went into seven printings, and Rube, who never forgot a partnership, split his share with Henrietta. I reckon that's the reason, when Dutch's son was born six months after his pa's death, she named the boy Reuben.

They're all of them gone now. The influenza took Henrietta in 1917, seven years to the day after Mary Elizabeth Treefall passed to her reward in the same house. I heard Ford Harper got himself stomped to death by a chestnut stallion on his little tenant place the day before the century turned. Nobody knows what become of Dick Leaping Deer, but it's a fair bet cannibals ate him if he wasn't hung or shot by some greaser lawman down there below the equator. And in 1905 they found Rube Belford slumped over a ledger in his office, his big old heart bust. They tell me half of Texas come out for the burying in the same cemetery where they planted the man who made him famous after the man was dead.

That there's the real story behind the death of Dutch Creel on Christmas Eve, 1899.

Don't look for it in no moving picture house anytime soon.

REUBEN CREEL
Treefall Ranch, Oklahoma March 12, 1924

THE BANDIT

They cut him loose a day early.

It worried him a little, and when the night captain on his block brought him a suit of clothes and a cardboard suitcase containing a toothbrush and a change of shirts, he considered bringing it up, but in that moment he suddenly couldn't stand it there another hour. So he put on the suit and accompanied the guard to the administration building, where the assistant warden made a speech, grasped his hand, and presented him with a check for $1,508. At the gate he shook hands with the guard, although the man was new to his section and he didn't know him, then stepped out into the gray autumn late afternoon. Not counting incarceration time before and during his trial, he had been behind bars twenty-eight years, eleven months, and twenty-nine days.

While he was standing there, blinking rapidly in

diffused sunlight that was surely brighter than that on the other side of the wall, a leather-bonneted assembly of steel and inflated rubber came ticking past on the street with a goggled and dustered operator at the controls. He watched it go by towing a plume of dust and blue smoke and said, "Oldsmobile."

He had always been first in line when magazines donated by the DAR came into the library, and while his fellow inmates were busy snatching up the new catalogs and finding the pages containing pictures of women in corsets and camisoles torn out, he was paging through the proliferating motoring journals, admiring the photographs and studying the technical illustrations of motors and transmissions. Gadgets had enchanted him since he saw his first steam engine aboard a Missouri River launch at age ten, and he had a fair idea of how automobiles worked. However, aside from one heart-thudding glimpse of the warden's new Locomobile parked inside the gates before the prison board decided its presence stirred unhealthy ambitions among the general population, this was his first exposure to the belching, clattering reality. He felt like a wolf whelp looking on the harsh glitter of the big world outside its parents' den for the first time.

After the machine had gone, he put down the suitcase to collect his bearings. In the gone days he had enjoyed an instinct for directions, but it had been replaced by other, more immediate survival mechanisms inside. Also, an overgrown village that had stood only two stories high on dirt streets as wide as pastures when he first came to it had broken out in brick towers and macadam and climbed the hills across the river, where an electrified trolley raced through a former cornfield clanging its bell like a mad mother cow. He wasn't sure if the train station would be where he left it in 1878.

He considered banging on the gate and asking the guard, but the thought of turning around now made him pick up his suitcase and start across the street at double-quick step, the mess-hall march. "The wrong way beats no way," Micah used to put it.

It was only a fifteen-minute walk, but for an old man who had stopped pacing his cell in 1881 and stretched his legs for only five of the twenty minutes allotted daily in the exercise yard, it was a hike. He had never liked walking anyway, had reached his majority breaking mixed-blood stallions that had run wild from December to March on the old Box W, and had done some of his best thinking and fighting with a horse under him. So when at last he reached the station, dodging more motorcars—the novelty of that wore off the first time—and trying not to look to passersby like a convict in his tight suit swinging a dollar suitcase, he was sweating and blowing like a wind-broke mare.

The station had a water closet—a closet indeed, with a gravity toilet and a mirror in need of resilvering over a white enamel basin, but a distinct improvement over the stinking bucket he had had to carry down three tiers of cells and dump into the cistern every morning for twenty-nine years. He placed the suitcase on the toilet seat, hung up his hat and soaked coat, unhooked his spectacles, turned back his cuffs, ran cold water into the basin, and splashed his face. Mopping himself dry on a comparatively clean section of roller towel, he looked at an old man's unfamiliar reflection, then put on his glasses to study it closer. But for the mirror in the warden's office it was the first one he'd seen since his trial; mirrors were made of glass, and glass was good for cutting wrists and throats. What hair remained on his scalp had gone dirty-gray. The flesh of his face was sagging, pulling away from the bone, and so pale he took a moment locating the bullet-crease on his forehead from Liberty. His beard was yellowed white, like stove grime. (All the men inside wore beards. It was easier than trying to shave without mirrors.) It was his grandfather's face.

Emerging from the water closet, he read the train schedule on the blackboard next to the ticket booth and checked it against his coin-battered old turnip watch, wound and set for the first time in half his lifetime. A train to Huntsford was pulling out in forty minutes.

He was alone at his end of the station with the ticket agent and a lanky young man in a baggy checked suit slouched on one of the varnished benches with his long legs canted out in front of him and his hands in his pockets. Conscious that the young man was watching him, but accustomed to being watched, he walked up to the booth and set down the suitcase. "Train to Huntsford on schedule?"

"Was last wire." Perched on a stool behind the window, the agent looked at him over the top of his *Overland Monthly* without seeing him. He had bright predatory eyes in a narrow face that had foiled an attempt to square it off with thick burnsicles. "How much to Huntsford?"

"Four dollars."

He unfolded the check for $1,508 and smoothed it out on the ledge under the glass. "I can't cash that," said the agent. "You'll have to go to the bank."

"Where's the bank?"

"Well, there's one on Treelawn and another on Cross. But they're closed till Monday."

"I ain't got cash on me."

"Well, the railroad don't offer credit."

While the agent resumed reading, he unclipped the big watch from its steel chain and placed it on top of the check. "How much you allow me on that?"

The agent glanced at it, then returned to his magazine. "This is a railroad station, not a jeweler's. I got a watch."

He popped open the lid and pointed out the engraving. "See that J.B.H.? That stands for James Butler Hickok. Wild Bill himself gave it to me when he was sheriff in Hays."

"Mister, I got a scar on my behind I can say I got from Calamity Jane, but I'd still need four dollars to ride to Huntsford. Not that I'd want to."

"Problem, Ike?"

The drawled question startled old eardrums thickened to approaching footsteps.

The young man in the checked suit was at his side, a head taller and smelling faintly of lilac water.

"Just another convict looking to wrestle himself a free ride off the C. H. & H.," the agent said. "Nothing I don't handle twice a month."

"What's the fare?"

The agent told him. The man in the checked suit produced a bent brown wallet off his right hip and counted four bills onto the window ledge.

"Hold up there. I never took a thing free off nobody that wasn't my idea to start."

"Well, give me the watch."

"This watch is worth sixty dollars."

"You were willing to trade it for a railroad ticket."

"I was not. I asked him what he'd give me on it."

"Sixty dollars for a gunmetal watch that looks like it's been through a thresher?"

"It keeps good time. You see that J.B.H.?"

"Wild Bill. I heard." The man in the checked suit counted the bills remaining in his wallet. "I've got just ten on me."

He closed the watch and held it out. "I'll give you my sister's address in Huntsford. You send me the rest there."

"You're trusting me? How long did you serve?"

"He's got a check drawn on the state bank for fifteen hundred," said the agent, separating a ticket from the perforated sheet.

The man in the checked suit pursed his lips. "Mister, you must've gone in there with some valuables. Last I knew, prison wages still came to a dollar a week."

"They ain't changed since I went in."

Both the ticket agent and the man in the checked suit were staring at him now. "Mister, you keep your watch. You've earned that break."

"It ain't broke, just dented some. Anyway, I said before I don't take charity."

"Let's let the four dollars ride for now. Your train's not due for a half hour. If I'm not satisfied with our talk at the end of that time, you give me it to hold and I'll send it on later, as a deposit against the four dollars."

"Folks paying for talking now?"

"They do when they've met someone who's been in prison since Hayes was president and all they've had to talk to today is a retiring conductor and a miner's daughter on her way to a finishing school in Chicago." The man in the checked suit offered his hand. "Arthur Brundage. I write for the New Democrat. It's a newspaper, since your time."

"I saw it inside." He grasped the hand tentatively, plainly surprising its owner with his grip, "I got to tell you, son, I ain't much for talking to the papers. Less people know your name, the less hold they got on you, Micah always said."

"Micah?"

He hesitated. "Hell, he's been dead better than twenty-five years, I don't reckon I can hurt him. Micah Hale. Maybe the name don't mean nothing now."

"These old cons, they'll tell you they knew John Wilkes Booth and Henry the Eighth if you don't shut them up." The ticket agent skidded the ticket across the ledge.

But Brundage was peering into his face now, a man trying to make out the details in a portrait fogged and darkened with years.

"You're Jubal Steadman."

"I was when I went in. I been called Dad so long I don't rightly answer to nothing else."

"Jubal Steadman." It was an incantation. "If I didn't fall in sheep dip and come up dripping double eagles. Let's go find a bench." Brundage seized the suitcase before its owner could get his hands on it and put a palm on his back, steering him toward the seat he himself had just vacated.

"The Hale-Steadman Gang," he said, when they were seated. "Floyd and Micah Hale and the Steadman brothers and Kid Stone. When I was ten, my mother found a copy of the New York Detective Monthly under my bed. It had Floyd Hale on the cover, blazing away from horseback with a six-shooter in each hand at a posse chasing him. I had to stay indoors for a week and memorize a different Bible verse every day."

Jubal smiled. His teeth were only a year old and he was just a few months past grinning like an ape all the time. "Then dime writers made out like Floyd ran the match, but that was just because the Pinkertons found out his name first and told the papers. We all called him Doc on account of he was always full of no-good clabber and he claimed to study eye doctoring back East for a year, when everyone knew he was in the Detroit House of Corrections for stealing a mall sack off a railroad hook. He told me I'd never need glasses." He took his off to polish them with a coarse handkerchief.

Brundage had a long notepad open on his knee. He stopped writing. "I guess I should have accepted that watch when you offered it."

"It ain't worth no sixty dollars. I got it off a fireman on the Katy Flyer when we hit it outside Choctaw in '73."

"You mean that was a story about Wild Bill?"

"Never met him. I had them initials put in it and made up the rest. It pulled me through some skinny times. Folks appreciated a good lie then, not like now."

"Readers of the *New Democrat* are interested in the truth."

He put his spectacles back on and peered at the journalist over the rims. But Brundage was writing again and missed it.

"Anyway, if there was someone we all looked to when things went sore, it was Doc's brother Micah. I reckon he was the smartest man I ever knew or ever will. That's why they took him alive and Doc let himself get shot in the back of the head by Kid Stone."

"I always wondered if he really did that just for the reward."

"I reckon. He was always spending his cut on yellow silk vests and gold hatbands. I was in prison two years when it happened so I can't say was that it. That blood money busted up all the good bunches. The Pinks spent years trying to undercut us with the hill folk, but it was the rewards done it in the end."

"The Kid died of pneumonia three or four years ago in New Jersey. He put together his own moving picture outfit after they let him go. He was playing Doc Holliday when he took sick."

"Josh always said Virge was a born actor. Virgil, that was the Kid's right name."

"I forget if Joshua was your older or your younger brother."

"Older. Billy Tom Mulligan stabbed him with a busted toothbrush first year we was inside. They hung him for it. Josh played the Jew's harp. He was playing it when they jumped us after Liberty."

"What really happened in Liberty?" Jubal pulled a face. "Doc's idea. We was to hit the ten-twelve from Kansas City when it stopped to water and take on passengers, and the bank in town at the same time.

We recruited a half dozen more men for the job: Creek Eddie, Charley MacDonald, Bart and Barney Dee, and two fellows named Bob and Bill, I never got their last names and couldn't tell which was which. Me and Josh and my kid brother Judah went with Micah and Charley MacDonald on the bank run and the rest took the train. Bart and Barney was to ride it in from Kansas City and sit on the conductor and porters while Doc and them threw down on the engineer and fireman and blew open the express car with powder. Doc said they wouldn't be expecting us to try it in town. He was dead-right there. No one thought we was that stupid."

"What made Micah go along with it?"

"Fambly bliss. Doc was threatening to take Kid Stone and start his own bunch because no one ever listened to them good plans he was coming up with all the time, like kidnapping the Governor of Missouri and holding him for ransom. Creek Eddie learned his trade in the Nations, so when he heard he was available, Micah figured he'd be a good influence on Doc. Meantime Creek Eddie thought the train thing was a harebrained plan but figured if Micah was saying yes to it, it must be all right." He showed his store teeth. "You see, I had twenty-nine years to work this all out, and if I knew it then—well, I wouldn't of had the twenty-nine years to work it all out.

"Micah and Charley and Josh and Judah and me, we slid through that bank like a grease fire and come out with seven thousand in greenbacks and another four or five thousand in securities. *And* the bank president and his tellers and two customers hollering for help on the wrong side of the vault door on a five-minute time lock. We never made a better or a quieter job. That was when we heard the shooting down at the station."

"A railroad employee fired the first shot, if I remember my reading."

"It doesn't matter who fired it. Bart and Barney Dee missed the train in Kansas City, and the conductor and a porter or two was armed and free when Doc and the rest walked in thinking the opposite. Creek Eddie got it in the back of the neck and hit the ground dead. Then everybody opened up, and by the time we showed with the horses, the smoke was all mixed up with steam from the boiler. Well, you could see your hand in front of your face, but not to shoot at. That didn't stop us, though.

"Reason was, right about then that time lock let loose of them folks we left in the bank, and when they hit the street yammering like bitch dogs, that whole town turned vigilante in a hot St. Louis minute. They opened up the gun shop and filled their pockets with cartridges and it was like Independence Day. I think as many of them fell in their own crossfire as what we shot.

"Even so, only six men was killed in that spree. If you was there trying to hold down your mount with one hand and twisting back and forth like a steam governor to fire on both sides of its neck and dodging all that lead clanging off the engine, you'd swear it was a hundred. I seen Charley take a spill and get dragged by his paint for twenty feet before he cleared his boot of the stirrup, and Judah got his jaw took off by a bullet, though he lived another eight or nine hours. Engineer was killed, and one rubberneck standing around waiting to board the train, and two of them damn fool townies playing Kit Carson on the street. I don't know how many of them was wounded; likely not as many as are still walking around showing off their old gallbladder scars as bullet-creases. I still got a ball in my back that tells me when it's fixing to rain, but that didn't give me as much trouble at the time as this here cut that kept dumping blood into my eyes." He pointed out the white mark where his hairline used to be. "Micah took one through the meat on his upper arm, and my brother Josh got it in the hip and lost a finger, and they shot the Kid and took him prisoner and arrested Charley, who broke his ankle getting loose of that stirrup. Doc was the only one of us that come away clean.

"Judah, his jaw was just hanging on by a piece of gristle. I tied it up with his bandanna, and Josh and me got him over one of the horses and we got mounted and took off one way while Doc and Micah and that Bill and Bob went the other. We met up at this empty farmhouse six miles north of town that we lit on before the job in case we got separated, all but that Bill and Bob. Them two just kept riding. We buried Judah that night."

"The posse caught up with you at the farmhouse?" asked Brundage, after a judicious pause.

"No, they surprised Josh and me in camp two nights later. We'd split with the Hales before then. Micah wasn't as bad wounded as Josh and we was slowing them down, Doc said. Josh could play that Jew's harp of his, though. Posse come on afoot, using the sound of it for a mark. They threw down on us. We gave in without a shot."

"That was the end of the Hale-Steadman Gang?"

A hoarse stridency shivered the air. In its echo, Jubal consulted his watch. "Train still runs on time. Nice to know some things stay the same. Yeah, the Pinks picked up Micah posing as a cattle-buyer in Denver a few months later. I heard he died of scarlatina inside. Charley MacDonald got himself shot to pieces escaping with Kid Stone and some others, but the Kid got clear and him and Doc put together a bunch and robbed a train or two and some banks until the Kid shot him. I reckon I'm what's left."

"I guess you can tell readers of the *New Democrat* there's no profit in crime."

"Well, there's profit and profit." He stood up, working the stiffness out of his joints, and lifted the suitcase.

Brundage hesitated in the midst of closing his notebook. "Twenty-nine years of your life a fair trade for a few months of excitement?"

"I don't reckon there's much in life you'd trade half of it to have. But in them days a man either broke his back and his heart plowing rocks under in some field or shook his brains loose putting some red-eyed horse to leather or rotted behind some counter in some town. I don't reckon I'm any older now than I would have been if I done any of them things to live. And I wouldn't have no youngster like you hanging on my every word neither. Them things become important when you get up around my age."

"I won't get that past my editor. He'll want a moral lesson."

"Put one in, then. It don't..." His voice trailed off.

The journalist looked up. The train was sliding to a stop inside the vaulted station, black and oily and leaking steam out of a hundred joints. But the old man was looking at the pair of men coming in the station entrance. One, sandy-haired and approaching middle age in a suit too heavy for Indian summer, his cherry face glistening, was the assistant warden at the prison. His companion was a city police officer in uniform. At sight of Jubal, relief blossomed over the assistant warden's features.

"Steadman, I was afraid you'd left." Jubal said, "I knew it."

As the officer stepped to the old man's side, the assistant warden said, "I'm very sorry. There's been a clerical error. You'll have to come back with us."

"I was starting to think you was going to let me have that extra day after all."

"Day?" The assistant warden was mopping his face with a lawn handkerchief. "I was getting set to close your file. I don't know how I overlooked that other charge." Jubal felt a clammy fist clench inside his chest. "Other charge?"

"For the train robbery. In Liberty. The twenty-nine years was for robbing the bank and for your part in the killings afterward. You were convicted also of accessory in the raid on the train. You have seventeen years to serve on that conviction, Steadman. I'm sorry."

He took the suitcase while the officer manacled one of the old man's wrists.

Brundage left the bench.

"Jubal—"

He shook his head. "My sister's coming in on the morning train from Huntsford tomorrow. Meet it, will you? Tell her."

"This isn't the end of it. My paper has a circulation of thirty thousand. When our readers learn of this injustice—"

"They'll howl and stomp and write letters to their congressmen, just like in '78."

The journalist turned to the man in uniform. "He's sixty years old. Do you have to chain him like a maniac?"

"Regulations." He clamped the other manacle around his own wrist.

Jubal held out his free hand. "I got to go home

now. Thanks for keeping an old man company for an hour."

After a moment Brundage took it. Then the officer touched the old man's arm and he blinked behind his spectacles and turned and left the station with the officer on one side and the assistant warden on the other. The door swung shut behind them.

As the train pulled out without Jubal, Brundage timed it absently against the dented watch in his hand.

THE TREE ON EXECUTION HILL

I t seemed as if everybody in Good Advice had turned out for the meeting that night in the town hall. Every seat was taken, and the dark oaken rafters hewn and fit in place by the ancestors of a good share of those present resounded with a steady hum of conversation while the broad pine planks that made up the floor creaked beneath the tread of many feet.

Up in front, his plaid jacket thrown back to expose a generous paunch, Carl Lathrop, the town's leading storekeeper and senior member of the council, stood talking with Birdie Flatt from the switchboard. His glasses flashed a Morse code in the bright overhead lights as he settled and resettled them on his fleshy nose. I recognized the gesture from the numerous interviews I had conducted with him as a sign that he was feeling very satisfied with himself, and so I knew what was coming long before most of my neighbors suspected it.

I was something of a freak in the eyes of the citizenry of Good Advice, New Mexico. This was partly because I had been the first person to settle in the area since before 1951, when the aircraft plant had moved on to greener pastures, and partly because, at 42, I was at least ten years younger than anyone else in town. Most people supposed I stayed on out of despair after my wife Sylvia left me to return to civilization, but that wasn't strictly true. We'd originally planned to lay over for a week or two while I collected information for my book and then move on. But then the owner of the town newspaper had died and the paper was put up for sale, and I bought it with the money we'd saved up for the trip. It had been an act of impulse, perhaps a foolish one—certainly it had seemed so to my wife, who had no intention of living so far away from her beloved beauty parlors—but my chief fear in life had always been that I'd miss the big opportunity when it came along. So now I had a newspaper but no Sylvia, which, all things considered, seemed like a pretty fair trade.

The buzz of voices died out as Lathrop took his place behind the lectern. I flipped open my notebook and sat with pencil poised to capture any pearls of wisdom he might have been about to drop.

"We all know why we're here, so we'll dispense with the long-winded introductions." A murmur of approval rippled through the audience. "You've all heard the rumor that the state may build a super-highway near Good Advice," he went on. "Well, it's my pleasant duty to announce that it's no longer a rumor."

Cheers and applause greeted this statement, and it was some minutes before the room grew quiet enough for Lathrop to continue.

"Getting information out of these government fellows is like pulling teeth," he said. "But after about a dozen phone calls to the capital, I finally got hold of the head of the contracting firm that's going to do the job. He told me they plan to start building sometime next fall." He waited until the fresh applause faded, then went on. "Now, this doesn't mean that Good Advice is going to become another Tombstone overnight. When those tourists come streaming in here, we're going to have to be ready for them. That means rezoning for tourist facilities, fixing up our historic landmarks, and so on. The reason we called this meeting is to decide on ways to make this town appealing to visitors. The floor is open to suggestions."

I spent the next twenty minutes jotting down some of the ideas that came from the enthusiastic citizens. Birdie Flatt was first, with a suggestion that the telephone service be updated, but others disagreed, maintaining that the old upright phones and wall installations found in many of the downtown shops added to the charm of the town. "Uncle Ned"

Scoffield, at 97 Good Advice's oldest resident, offered to clean out and fix up the old trading post at the end of Main Street in return for permission to sell his wood carvings and his collection of hand-woven Navajo rugs. Carl Lathrop pledged to turn the old jail, which he had been using as a storeroom, into a tourist attraction. The fact that outlaw Ford Harper had spent his last days there before his hanging, he said, could only add to its popularity. Then, amid a chorus of groans from scattered parts of the room, Avery Sharecross stood up.

Sharecross was a spindly scarecrow of a man, with an unkempt mane of lusterless black hair spilling over the collar of his frayed sweater and a permanent stoop that made him appear much older than he was. Nobody in town could say how he made his living. Certainly not from the bookstore he had been operating on the corner of Main and Maple for thirty years; there were never any more than two customers in the store at a time, and the prices he charged were so ridiculously low that it was difficult to believe that he managed to break even, let alone show a profit. Everyone was aware of the monthly pension he received from an address in Santa Fe, but no one knew how much it was or why he got it. His bowed shoulders and shuffling gait, the myopia that forced him to squint through the thick lenses of his eyeglasses, the hollows in his pale cheeks were as much a part of the permanent scenery in Good Advice as the burned-out shell of the old flour mill north of town. I closed my notebook and put away my pencil, knowing what he was going to talk about before he opened his mouth. It was all he ever talked about.

Lathrop sighed. "What is it, Avery? As if I didn't know." He rested his chin on one pudgy hand, bracing himself for the ordeal.

"Mr. Chairman, I have a petition." The old bookseller rustled the well-thumbed sheaf of papers he held in one talonlike hand. "I have twenty-six signatures demanding that the citizens of Good Advice vote on whether the tree on Execution Hill be removed."

There was an excited buzz among the spectators. I sat bolt upright in my chair, flipping my notebook back open. How had the old geezer got twenty-five people to agree with him?

For 125 years the tree in question had dominated the high-domed hill two miles outside of town, its skeletal limbs stretching naked against the sky. Of the eighteen trials that had been held in the town hail during the last century, eleven of those tried had ended up swinging from the tree's stoutest limb. It was a favorite spot of mine, an excellent place to sit and meditate. Avery Sharecross, for reasons known only to himself, had been trying to get the council to destroy it for five years. This was the first time he had not stood alone.

Lathrop cleared his throat loudly, probably to cover up his own astonishment. "Now, Avery, you know as well as I do that it takes fifty-five signatures on a petition to raise a vote. You've read the charter."

Sharecross was unperturbed. "When that charter was drafted, Mr. Chairman, this town boasted a population of over fourteen hundred. In the light of our present count, I believe that provision can be waived." He struck the pages with his finger-tips. "These signatures represent nearly one-tenth of the local voting public. They have a right to be heard."

"How come you're so fired up to see that tree reduced to kindling, anyway? What's the difference to your?"

"That tree"—Sharecross flung a scrawny arm in the direction of the nearest window—"represents a time in this town's history when lynch law reigned and pompous hypocrites sentenced their peers to death regardless of their innocence or guilt." His cheeks were flushed now, his eyes ablaze behind the bottle-glass spectacles. "That snarl of dead limbs has been a blemish on the smooth face of this community for over a hundred years, and it's about time we got rid of it."

It was an impressive performance, and he sounded sincere, but I wasn't buying it.

Good Advice, after all, had not been my first exposure to journalism. After you've been in this business awhile, you get a feeling for when someone is telling the truth, and Sharecross wasn't. Whatever reasons he had for wishing to destroy the town's oldest landmark, they had nothing to do with any sense of injustice. Of that I was certain.

Lathrop sighed. "All right, Avery, let's see your petition. If the signatures check out, we'll vote." Once the papers were in his hands, Lathrop called the other members of the town council around him to look them over. Finally he motioned them back to their seats and turned back toward the lectern. For the next half hour he read off the names on the petition—many of which surprised me, for they included some of the town's leading citizens—to make sure the signatures were genuine. Every one of those mentioned spoke up to assure him that they were. At length the storekeeper laid the pages down.

"Before we vote," he said, "the floor is open to dissenting opinions—Mr. Macklin?"

My hand had gone up before he finished speaking. I got to my feet, conscious of all the eyes upon me. "No one is arguing what Mr. Sharecross said about the injustices done in the past," I began haltingly. "But tearing down something that's a large part of our history won't change anything." I paused, searching for words. I was a lot more eloquent behind a typewriter. "Mr. Sharecross says the tree reminds us of the sordid past. I think that's as it should be. A nagging reminder of a time when we weren't so noble is a healthy thing to have in our midst. I wouldn't want to live in a society that kicked its mistakes under the rug."

The words were coming easier now. "There's

been a lot of talk here tonight about promoting tourist trade. Well, destroying a spot where eleven infamous badmen met their reward is one sure way of aborting any claims we might have had upon shutter- happy visitors." I shook my head emphatically, a gesture left over from my college debating-club days. "History is too precious for us to turn our backs on it, for whatever reason. Sharecross and his sympathizers would do well to realize that our true course calls for us to turn our gaze forward and forget about rewriting the past."

There was some applause as I sat down, but it died out when Sharecross seized the floor again. "I'm not a philistine, Mr. Chairman," he said calmly. "Subject to the will of the council, I hereby pledge the sum of five thousand dollars for the erection of a statue of Enoch Howard, Good Advice's founder, atop Execution Hill once the tree has been removed. I, too, have some feeling for history." His eyes slid in my direction.

That was dirty pool, I thought as he took his seat amid thunderous cheering from those present. In one way or another, Enoch Howard's blood flowed in the veins of over a third of the population of Good Advice. Now I knew how he had obtained those signatures. But why? What did he hope to gain?

"What about expense?" someone said.

"No problem," countered Sharecross, on his feet again. "Floyd Kramer there has offered to bulldoze down the tree and cart it away at cost."

"That true, Floyd?" Lathrop asked.

A heavy-jowled man in a blue work shirt buttoned to the neck gave him the high sign from his standing position near the door.

I shot out of my chair again, but this time my eyes were directed upon my skeletal opponent and not the crowd. "I've fought you in print and on the floor of the town hall over this issue," I told him, "and if necessary I'll keep on fighting you right to the top of Execution Hill. I don't care how many statues you pull out of your hat; you won't get away with whatever it is you're trying to do."

The old bookseller made no reply. His eyes were blank behind his spectacles. I sat back down.

I could see that Lathrop's attitude had changed, for he had again taken to raising and lowering his eyeglasses confidently upon the bridge of his nose. Enoch Howard was his great-grandfather on his mother's side. "Now we'll vote," he said. "All those in favor of removing the tree on Execution Hill to make room for a statue of Enoch Howard signify by saying aye."

Rain was hissing on the grass when I parked my battered pickup truck at the bottom of the hill and got out to fetch the shovel out of the back. It was a long climb to the top and I was out of shape, but I didn't want to risk leaving telltale ruts behind by driving up the slope. Halfway up my feet began to feel like lead and the blood was pounding in my ears like a pneumatic hammer; by the time I found myself at the base of the deformed tree I had barely enough energy left to find the spot I wanted and begin digging. It was dark, and the soil was soaked just enough so that each time I took out a shovelful the hole filled up again, with the result that it was ten minutes before I made any progress at all. After half an hour I stopped to rest. That's when all the lights came on and turned night into day.

The headlights of half a dozen automobiles were trained full upon me. For a fraction of a second I stood unmoving, frozen with shock. Then I hurled the shovel like a javelin at the nearest light and started to run. The first step I took landed in the hole. I fell headlong to the ground, emptying my lungs and twisting my ankle painfully. When I looked up, I was surrounded by people.

"I've waited five years for this." The voice belonged to Avery Sharecross. "How did you know?" I said when I found my breath.

"I never did. Not for sure." Sharecross was standing over me now, an avenging angel wearing a threadbare coat and scarf. "I once heard that you spent all the money you had on the newspaper. If that was true, I wondered what your wife used for bus fare back to Santa Fe when she left you. Everyone knew you argued with her bitterly over your decision to stay. That you lost control and murdered her seemed obvious to me.

"I decided you buried her at the foot of the hanging tree, which was the reason you spent more time here than anyone else. The odds weren't in favor of my obtaining permission to dig up the hill because of mere supposition, so it became necessary to catch you in the act of unearthing her yourself. That's when I got the idea to propose removing the tree and force you to find someplace else to dispose of the body."

He turned to a tall man whose Stetson glistened wetly in the unnatural illumination of the headlights at his back. "Sheriff, if your men will resume digging where Mr. Macklin left off, it's my guess you'll find the corpse of Sylvia Macklin before morning. I retired from the Santa Fe Police Department long before they felt the need to teach us anything about reading rights to those we arrested, so perhaps you'll oblige."

THE ANGEL OF SANTA SOFIA

The Pinkerton was a lean kid with a rusty fringe along his upper lip and a passion for plaid vests and tequila taken without salt and buxom, dark-eyed senoritas twice his age. He was working on one at his table now, who he claimed was involved with a case, but her bedroom eyes and the fierce glances the couple was drawing from a mustachioed Mexican at the bar said different. Well, he was old enough to take care of himself.

"I hate to keep interrupting," I told him patiently, "but I've come six hundred miles and I'd sort of like to be reassured that it wasn't for nothing."

"Who'd you say you were again?" He sipped his tequila without taking his eyes from the handsome *mujer*.

I laid the badge, which I never wear, atop the warrant I'd been carrying since Montana. "Page Murdock, deputy US marshal. Ten days ago you wired Judge Blackthorne in Helena that you had Dale Sykes under surveillance here in Santa Sofia. Where is he?"

"In a mission down by the river." He had scarcely glanced at either of the items. "You can't miss him. He fits the description on that dodger you had out on him."

Some persuasion seemed in order. I was muddy with dust and perspiration and exhausted from eighteen straight hours in the saddle, not counting the other one hundred and sixty I had spent there over the past ten days. I drew my English revolver from its holster and clanked it down in front of him. "Show me."

He gave the weapon rather more attention than he had my other credentials. Then he signed, kissed his disappointed companion's hand, and snatched his plug hat from the table.

A short ride from town found us on a rise overlooking an adobe chapel awash in the old gold rays of the setting sun. The only things stirring in the yard were a tobacco- colored dog yawning and stretching from a day spent dozing in whatever shade was available and a couple of Yaqui Indians busy rehanging the building's arched oaken door. We had been watching for about ten minutes when a figure in a brown hooded robe came out past them carrying a bucket in the direction of the river. The Pinkerton, whose name was Walsh, pointed at him.

"You're joking," I said.

He shook his head. "He's Sykes, down to the stiff elbow and strawberry mark on his left cheek. Around here he's known as Brother Dale. The locals know who he is and what he's done and don't care."

"It's wonderful what a little money can do. The conductor he shot in that mail train robbery two years ago is still chained to a bed. He'll be there the rest of his life."

"As I understand it," said Walsh, "there's no money involved. According to the townspeople I questioned, a local farmer found him lying beside the road a mile north of here about two weeks after the robbery. He had four bullets in him. There isn't a doctor for a hundred miles, so he was taken to the old padre. He was delirious by that time, and it wasn't long before everyone knew his life history. The padre calls his recovery a miracle. The Yaquis think tequila had more to do with it. At any rate, instead of heading down across the border as expected when he was strong enough, Sykes paid for his keep by doing odd jobs around the mission, fixing things up, things like that. Claimed he had seen the light. Last year he was at the river washing that brown robe the padre gave him when a little girl playing along the bank fell in. He jumped in and saved her from drowning. Since then he's been something of a folk hero hereabouts."

I squinted through the failing light at the man kneeling on the riverbank. His stiffened right elbow was made obvious by the way he manipulated the bucket while filling it. The bone had been shattered by a bullet during a shoot-out at a botched-up bank robbery five years before. "This is going to be easier than I thought," I said.

"That's what you think," snorted the Pinkerton. "As far as the people of Santa Sofia are concerned, he's an angel."

"Angels fall."

The sheriff, a dark, thickset Mexican who shooed his wife and daughters away from the dinner table while he spoke to us, had a habit of waving both arms over his head when agitated, which appeared to be his normal state. He became even more so when I requested his assistance in arresting Dale Sykes.

"*Lo siento, señores!*" he cried, narrowly missing the coal-oil lamp suspended from the ceiling with a flying right hand. "This is something I cannot do. The election, she is but *tres semanas*—three weeks— away. To help apprehend the most popular man since Miguel Hidalgo would be to commit what you norteamericanos would call political suicide. I will let you house him in my jail, as no peace officer can refuse another the use of his facilities, but I dare not go further."

I could have persuaded him to co-operate, but it was obvious that he would have been worse than no support at all. I did get him to lend me a pair of horses from the string of three he kept in a corral behind his home, left my own exhausted mount to the care of his son-in-law, and with Walsh riding beside me and the third horse in tow I returned to the mission.

No guards were posted out front and the door was unlocked. Inside, the chapel was a cavern saved from absolute blackness by a hundred tiny flames that danced wildly in the disturbed air. One of the flames at the far end was moving, propelled by the hand of an old man standing behind the altar, who was busy lighting candles with a long taper. He wore a robe like the one we had seen on Sykes, with the hood thrown back to reveal a head of colorless hair curling over a black skull cap and a face like ancient oilcloth. Bright eyes observed our approach.

"I am Father Mendoza. May I help you?" As he spoke, his wasted features leaped into sudden prominence as if illuminated by his Holy Spirit, but it was only the reflected glow of the flaming taper as he brought it to his lips. He blew it out.

I showed the badge. He nodded sadly. "He told me you would come."

"God?" asked Walsh.

"Brother Dale. He said that someday men would come to take him back to atone for his sins."

"Where is he?" I demanded. Piety brings out my bad side.

"In the back. Firearms will not be necessary."

I ignored him, drawing my gun as I strode toward the arch dimly outlined in the back wall. A tremendous bulk blocked my path. I looked up into the stern features of one of the Yaquis I had seen at work in the yard earlier. "Call him off," I told Mendoza. "Before his blood defiles the sanctity of the Church."

"For God's sake, Murdock!" breathed the Pinkerton. "Let him pass, Diego," Mendoza said.

The Indian stepped inside with a grunt and I pushed past, Walsh at my heels. We were in a dank corridor, heavy with mildew and lit only by a pale glow beyond a hall- open door to the right. There were two others, both closed. I chose the open one.

Dale Sykes, looking much as he had in the old rotogravure Judge Blackthorne had distributed among the marshals, only heavier and more sinister with the strawberry mark on his cheek an angry red blaze, was seated on the edge of a stone pallet strewn not too generously with straw, reading a worn Bible in the light of a candle guttering on a rickety table at his elbow. He too had peeled back his hood, exposing a skull cap and a wealth of ill-kept black hair. He looked up as we entered and made a move toward the book with his clumsy right arm.

"Stop!" My bellow rang off the walls of the cramped cell. "Get that Bible."

Walsh glanced at me strangely, but stepped forward and wrenched the black-bound volume from Syke's hand.

"I was only marking my place," said the man on the pallet.

I accepted the Bible and riffled through it while Walsh covered Sykes with a baby Remington he had taken from a special pocket beneath his left arm. The book had no hollow where a gun could be hidden. I tossed it onto the pallet. "Keep him covered while I search him," I told the Pinkerton.

There was nothing on him but a small belt purse containing a few coins. "Who shot you?" I asked him.

"My partners." His tone was low, apologetic. "We argued about how to divide the money from the mail train job. I lost, and they left me for dead."

"The same way you left that conductor," I said.

"He didn't die? Each night I pray that he did not."

"I'm sure he prays every night that he did. Get going." I moved away from the front door and waved him toward it with my gun.

The sheriff, who lived across the alley from the jail, muttered a string of gentle blasphemies in Spanish as he unlocked the door to the only cell. The key grated. Jails don't get a lot of use in border towns. When it was open I shoved the prisoner stumbling over the iron cot in the corner.

"There's no call to be so rough," the Pinkerton protested.

"We'll keep an eye on him tonight if it's all right with you," I told the sheriff. "If that son-in-law of yours is any good with horses we'll be able to pull out in the morning."

"What do you mean, 'we'?" Walsh's embryonic mustache bristled.

"The Great Northern Pacific has placed a thousand dollars on Sykes's head. I thought you might want to split it."

He made no reply.

We were interrupted only once during our vigil, when someone rapped on the front door. I came up out of a sound sleep on the sheriff's cot, drawing my gun. Walsh, who was standing first watch, was at the door with his Remington in hand. "Who is it?"

There was a muffled response. The Pinkerton opened the door and stepped back, displaying the gun. A short Mexican with a drawn, tragic face, attired in the sandals and shapeless white cotton shirt and trousers that comprise the male uniform down there, moved inside timidly, sombrero clutched in both hands. Just before Walsh closed the door behind him I caught a glimpse of a crowd of men in similar costumes and drably clad women gathered in front of the building.

In a voice scarcely above a whisper, our visitor said, "I have come, good *señores,* to petition for Brother Dale's release."

Walsh snorted. I said, "Who are you?"

"Francisco Vargas, *Señor* Marshal. I am the man whose little daughter Brother Dale rescued from the river last year. Because of this it was decided that I speak for the citizens of Santa Sofia."

"The whole town's with you on this?" I was standing over him now. He was trembling. He was old enough to remember Maximilian, and the days when all authority was considered evil.

"Go home, Francisco." Sykes had both hands on the bars of his cell. "I have sinned and must accept my punishment. Go home and tell everyone else to do the same."

"Herinano Dale!" Vargas stepped toward the prisoner. Their hands were almost touching when I lunged and sent the Mexican reeling with a back-hand slash across his face.

"Murdock!" cried Walsh, outraged. He thrust his revolver at me. I leveled mine. He stopped.

"Search him!" I snapped, indicating the Mexican cowering across the room. "That sombrero alone could hide an arsenal."

Somewhat subdued, the Pinkerton put away his gun and turned to the task. When he was finished he fixed me with an accusing glare. "He's not carrying so much as a nail file."

A stone crashed through the barred window in the door. Angry shouts drifted in through the jagged aperture.

"Now you've done it!" Walsh barked.

I flung an arm around Vargas's neck and dragged him into the center of the room. "Tell them if they aren't gone in five minutes I'll scatter your brains!" I placed the muzzle of my revolver against his right temple.

He did as directed. I remembered enough Spanish from my cowpunching days to know that nothing slipped past me. Walsh, watching at the window, told me when the last of the spectators had left. I let the Mexican go with the assurance that further incidents would mean Sykes's life, and took the next watch without comment. That seemed to suit the Pinkerton.

Dawn found the sheriff conspicuously absent, which was more than I could say for the rest of the town. It was out in force as we marched our prisoner out to where the son-in-law waited with our horses and the one I had bought from the sheriff the night before. I tossed the young man a five-dollar gold piece for their care and was ordering Sykes to mount up when a Mexican girl of about ten stepped out of the crowd bearing flowers "por *el Hermano Dale.*" I saw Francisco Vargas standing nearby and knew who she was.

"No gifts," I said, stepping between her and Sykes.

An angry murmuring arose from the crowd.

"Please," said Sykes, "may I speak to her?"

"Don't you have a heart?" Walsh demanded. "Let him."

I looked the girl over. "Just a second," I said, and tore the flowers from her grasp. I pulled apart the paper wrapping. Flowers fluttered to the ground, nothing more. The crowd laughed nastily. "Make it quick," I snapped.

The girl was crying. Bending over her, Sykes said a few soothing words in Spanish and raised a hand to tuck a stray tendril of hair into her scarf. He fanned his fingers, made a fist beside her ear, and asked her to hold out her hand. When she did so, four coins dropped into it from his fist. She laughed delightedly. He kissed her and turned toward his horse.

"Where'd you pick that up?" I demanded. "My father taught it to me. The children love it."

We left Santa Sofia at a trot, Sykes in the middle. Walsh reined in after half a mile. "What's the matter?" I drew rein. "Are we being followed?"

"No, and we're not likely to be. I'm going back."

"Meaning?"

"Meaning I don't like your kind of law, Murdock." His face was flushed. "This isn't the same man who robbed that mail train two years ago. His name may be Sykes and it may have been his finger that pulled the trigger on that conductor, but he isn't the same. But that doesn't make any difference to you, does it?"

"Is it supposed to?"

He looked at me sadly. "If you don't know the answer to that, you're beyond help."

"Suit yourself. Las Cruces is full of good men with guns who'll be willing to help collect that reward."

He wheeled and cantered off without another word.

———

A handful of lights were still burning in Santa Sofia as I rode ploddingly down its only street, leading the second horse with its burden slung across the saddle. As I neared the sheriff's home, a fresh yellow glow spread from one of the windows. The lawmen emerged carrying a shotgun and struggling to tug his suspenders up over his red-flanneled shoulders. "*Señor* Deputy!" he called. I kept going.

Another figure came trotting out the door of the cantina. This proved to be Walsh. "Murdock, what is it?" He took hold of my bridle. "What are you doing back? You just left this morning."

A crowd was gathering. A lantern was produced and the dead man on the other horse was examined. "It is Brother Dale!" someone exclaimed. There was an ominous rumbling.

"You killed him!" Walsh looked horrified.

"He pulled a gun," I said. "Ten miles north of here. He got off a shot. So did I. I didn't miss."

"He has been shot in the back!" said the sheriff.

"His horse panicked. He was turning to rein it back around when I plugged him." I had to shout to be heard above the furious babble of voices.

The Pinkerton was livid. "You're not only a murderer, but a liar as well! Where would he get a gun?"

"I wondered about that too. I think Vargas passed it to him last night just before I jumped him. You saw Sykes's sleight-of-hand trick with the coins. He could have plucked it out of the sombrero just as easily without us seeing him and hidden it out until it would do him the most good."

"Hogwash! You hated him and took advantage of the first opportunity to kill him. You'll hang for this, Murdock, badge or no badge!"

"Then why did I come back?" While he was puzzling that one out, I drew my revolver. "Let go of that bridle."

He obeyed. "Where are you going?"

"To the mission."

The whole town had turned out by the time I reached the chapel, shouting *"Asesino!"* and brandishing machetes and pitchforks. The padre and the two Yaquis were standing in the front. I had to back inside, rotating the gun right and left. I don't remember if I had cleared the threshold before I collapsed.

Later, Father Mendoza told me he'd taken twenty-seven stitches in the gash Brother Dale's bullet had carved along the right side of my rib cage.

ROSSITER'S STAND

The bone pickers started me thinking about Chris Rossiter for the first time in years. Dressed in rags, the family combing the tall grass for buffalo bones to be sold for use in refining sugar and making china was a fleeting image as my train highballed between Fargo and Bismark, but they lingered in memory as clearly as the details of that last day in Wyoming in the spring of 1872. It had been more than a decade, and yet in the luxury of my Pullman I could still feel the springless wagon lurching beneath me and smell the stench of green hides in back. Mine had been the filthy job of following the hunters—"runners," we called them—reining in beside each fresh-killed buffalo, making the necessary incisions at the neck, hoofs and belly, then hitching the wagon up to the hide and using horse power to peel it from the carcass. For this I received one-third of the take, sharing with Rossiter and Al

Decker, the runners, after wages were paid the Crow Indian guide who led us to the buffalo.

It was good money. The hides sold for $2.50 each and we averaged twenty kills a day over the six-month season. But that wasn't enough for Rossiter.

"It eats my guts out having to let so many of 'em go," he complained one evening as we sat around the campfire, digesting hump steaks and sipping strong coffee laced with good Irish whiskey, one of Rossiter's many conceits. He was a big man, rawboned, with a square, clean-shaven jaw and albino-blond eyebrows that stood out like chalk against his sunburned flesh. He wore buckskins and an eagle feather in his hat because he had read once in a dime novel that that was how buffalo runners dressed. Our first season was almost over and we had yet to meet anyone in similar costume. "If Hurley would step up his skinning," he went on, "we could bag a couple of hundred a day."

"Maybe you'd like to give him a hand with them," I snarled.

We were at this point in an extended confinement at which a chance remark that would have passed without notice a few weeks earlier could trigger violence. We glared at each other across the fire, the Indian watching us from the vantage point of an alien race. The Crow was small for a plains tribesman, dark as a rifle stock, and though he knew English at least as well as German-born Al Decker, he used words the way a man stranded in the desert rations water. His eyes were shadowed under his jutting brow.

Decker broke the spell. "Why bother, Chris?" He poured a fresh slug from Rossiter's flask into his tin cup. "We are rich men."

"We could be richer. I almost had a stand today."

Chris Rossiter talked in his sleep nights about having a stand. Legend had it that given the right conditions, a herd of grazing buffalo could be picked off piecemeal without stampeding, so long as none of them went down bawling.

"What good would that do?" I countered. "You'd kill too many to skin. We'd be leaving more hides than we took."

"That's what I'm talking about. You're too slow."

"And you're kill-crazy, just like those wolves that swarm around the carcasses at night. I was up past midnight flaying that batch you took yesterday because you couldn't stop."

Rising suddenly, he unsheathed the skinning knife he never used but kept razor-sharp. "Don't call me crazy."

I started to get up. Decker placed a hand on my thigh, stopping me.

"Let it go, Chris." His tone was soothing.

"Why should I?" Rossiter's face was hidden in darkness, but his entire frame was quivering with rage.

"Because you want to have grandchildren."

The muzzle of Decker's Spencer carbine peeped out from under the blanket he was sitting on.

That ended the discussion. A stout man whose good nature shone from a round face framed by reddish mutton-chop whiskers, Decker alone knew what it was like to kill a man, having served in the Franco-Prussian War. Rossiter put away his weapon reluctantly and we all turned in. But that night I slept with my own rifle close at hand.

We had scarcely broken camp the next day when the Indian signaled from horseback at the top of a low hill a quarter mile west. It was one of those mornings God seems to save up for all winter long, when the scraped blue of the sky is so bright and the air so clear you can make out the details on a mountain a hundred miles away.

Rossiter and Decker joined the Crow astride their mounts and I rumbled up last in the wagon. I had started to speak when the German reached down from his saddle and squeezed my arm. He was watching some three hundred buffalo grazing the broad plain that lay at the foot of the slope.

From dun to black they claimed all the subtle shades in between, the shaggy males brushing the ground with their beards and pretending to be in charge while their smoother and smaller mates awaited the crisis that would require their own leadership. Some were kneeling, but most were on their feet and munching at last year's grass where it had begun to straighten among receding patches of snow.

The sound of three hundred pairs of jaws turning tough grass into fodder was like the tramp of infantry.

Taking his time, Rossiter picketed his mount, sank the sharp end of a forked rest he carried with him into the ground and stretched out on his stomach behind it, nesting the barrel of his Sharps rifle in the crotch. He took a deep breath, released half of it, and touched off the first round with a deafening boom.

A puff of dust erupted behind the shoulder of a great bull standing on the edge of the herd. It grunted and folded down with tragic grace. The animals in the herd milled restlessly, but there was no mad rush.

The runner reloaded and fired again. Another bull collapsed, more quietly than the first, its tongue dusty pink against the snow.

The third time a cow snorted, rolled over, kicked and lay still. A yearling grazing nearby turned its great head to stare dumbly at the dead beast, then resumed feeding.

"Have you ever seen its like?" whispered Decker. He had dismounted but had made no move toward his own weapon.

"Why aren't you shooting?" I asked him. "This is Rossiter's stand."

The Indian squatted next to his horse, watching the slaughter in silence. The wind stirred the feathers in his pompadour; but for that he might have been carved out of the hilltop.

The morning went on, and dark mounds sprin-kled the landscape. When Rossiter's gun barrel grew too hot Decker handed him his Spencer and he used that for an hour, pacing his reloading to allow the metal time to cool. By then his own rifle was ready. When there were sixty dead buffalo on the plain I approached him.

"That's enough, Rossiter. I'll be all night skinning them as it is."

The last word was drowned beneath a fresh report. A baffle-scarred bull went down, vomiting dark blood.

"Did you hear me?" I demanded.

He was busy reloading. "I'm not deaf."

"I'll never be able to do them all."

"Then don't." He sighted in on a gray-humped loner standing two hundred yards from the others and dropped it with a breast shot.

The money we'd clear on what hides I could take meant less to him than the pile of spent shells that covered nearly every square inch of ground within two feet of him. My stomach did a slow turn. I stepped to the wagon and jerked my rifle from under the seat.

"Damn it, stop!"

For the time it took the echo of his last shot to crackle away into the distance, everyone's attention was on me and the muzzle I had trained on the reclining marksman. Then, with a supreme show of contempt, Rossiter turned his head away, plucked out the empty cartridge, replaced it, and resumed shooting.

I'll never know if I would have shot him because he had killed No. 72 when the herd spooked.

They were like birds deserting a tree. One moment they were grazing peacefully, oblivious to the steady decimation. The next they were all on their feet and fleeing. Great choking clouds of dust swept over us. The ground trembled.

Rossiter sprang up, Sharps in hand. "What the hell?"

A shot crashed. Decker cried out and fell.

Seven riders galloped at us through the haze of dust on the plain, waving rifles and yip-yapping like a pack of mongrels. They wore breastplates of pieced-together bone and their faces were painted red and black.

"Cheyenne!" Rossiter shouldered his rifle, but he was slower than our Crow guide, who had unslung his Henry and began hammering away at the advancing line. A brave whose face was decorated to resemble a death's head shrieked and cartwheeled off his horse's back.

I snatched up my rifle and fired three times rapidly. Everyone went wild. Beside me, Rossiter drew careful bead on an Indian with a buffalo-horn headdress and spilled him. At that point we doubled fire, the Crow loosing three shots in the time it took me to lever in a fresh round. As an age-old enemy of the Cheyenne he knew what to expect in the event we were defeated. Lead was thick around them when they finally got their rearing horses turned around and fled, still whooping. We stitched up the earth around them for good measure.

"Good shooting," gasped Decker, on the ground. "They aren't used to that kind of marksmanship from buffalo butchers."

He had taken a bullet in his right thigh. I got out my ripping knife and slit his trousers leg to get at it.

"Heathens." Rossiter reloaded with nervous fingers. "Spoiling a man's stand for the pure hell of it."

I said, "They have to live off the animal we kill just for the hide."

"Who says they got to live?"

Just then I glimpsed the Crow's face, distorted with a kind of hatred I had never seen in a White man's features. He caught me looking and his stoic expression returned as quickly as the buffalo had left.

The bullet had carried off some meat without stopping. I cleaned and dressed the wound from the medical kit and made Decker sip from the laudanum bottle. The opium and alcohol distillate eased the pain almost immediately. I tucked him into his bedroll and told Rossiter to look after him while I went about skinning the phenomenal kill.

"What about the Indians?" Rossiter demanded.

"Not be back today," said the Crow. "Mourn dead."

The Crow came along as my assistant. But for a meal break at sundown, we worked through till dawn, using lanterns for light. When we got back to camp, slick with perspiration and staggering, Rossiter was gone.

"He left at first light," said Decker over his morning laudanum. "He said something about showing that party of bucks a thing or two."

"He die," the Crow declared.

After two hours of sleep the Indian and I began staking the hides out to dry. We were nearly finished when he called my attention to a lone rider approaching through gathering dusk. It was Rossiter, slouched in the saddle and caked from crown to heel with a mud of sweat and dust. In camp he dismounted heavily.

"Followed them as far as the river," he said, undoing his cinch. "Then their tracks linked up with the trail of a hundred riders, maybe more. I wasn't about to take on the whole Cheyenne nation."

I was changing Decker's bandages. "We're going back tomorrow anyway. The season's over for us."

"One more day."

"Why? There's no room in the wagon for any more hides. Besides, I'm sick of buffalo and wide open spaces. I want to spend a night in a room with a real bed."

"You've waited this long."

"What about Decker? He needs a doctor."

"He's come through worse."

"Damn you, all you care about is getting another stand."

He made no reply.

Dawn was a pale promise when Rossiter stood and tossed the rest of the coffee in his cup into the fire. "Let's go, Indian."

"Leave him here," I said. "We only got through pegging those hides three hours ago."

"Indians don't need sleep." They mounted and left.

Decker had a bad morning. I was wondering whether to risk increasing his laudanum ration when the Crow returned. His face was a blank slab.

"Cheyenne attack. Rossiter dead."

Despite my protests, Decker insisted upon riding along to investigate. I helped him into his saddle. On the way, the Crow explained that Rossiter had been working a stand when a dozen braves stampeded the herd as before, shouting and firing. One of the shots struck Rossiter in the head. The guide had taken advantage of the dust raised by the charging herd to flee.

There were no Indians in sight when we arrived. The dead runner lay on his stomach on a low rise, his finger still curled around the trigger of his Sharps propped on its rest. I counted sixteen buffalo carcasses scattered across the surrounding grass.

Decker dismounted awkwardly and used his carbine as a crutch to hobble over to the corpse. A blue-black hole marred the smooth brown expanse of Rossiter's sunburned forehead.

"How close were the Cheyenne when he was killed?" asked the German.

The Indian shrugged. "Two hundred yard."

Decker nodded. "Cover him."

I stared. He repeated the directive. Puzzled, I raised my rifle. The Crow watched us through slits dried and cracked by prairie sun. Deep lines curved from his nostrils to the corners of his broad mouth.

"There are powder burns all around the wound," Decker said. "He was shot at close range, not from two hundred yards away."

"You're sure?"

"I have seen enough dead men to know."

"But if the Crow killed him," I said, "why didn't Rossiter defend himself? The Indian had to be standing right in front of."

A furrow of doubt appeared in the German's brow. "Tie him up. We will let the judge in Rock Springs work it out."

I hesitated. The Crow seized that moment to spring onto his horse's back. "Shoot him!" shouted Decker.

I shouldered the rifle, but paused with my finger hugging the trigger. The Indian smacked reins across his mount's neck and was gone in a dusty swirl. Decker leaned back against the wagon and swung up his Spencer. I tore it out of his hands.

"You'll blow your head off!" I cried. "The barrel's full of dirt."

By that time the Indian had vanished between hills. When he reappeared atop the next he was hopelessly out of range. I lowered my rifle. Turning, I met Al Decker's gaze. I still see it from time to time.

We didn't speak after that, except to exchange essential information. We buried Rossiter where he had fallen, cleared a handsome profit on the hides and parted company in Rock Springs, where I had seen Decker into a doctor's care. He didn't say good-bye. I never saw him again, though I heard that he bought into a trading post in Montana and married an Arapaho squaw. My end went into an education in law which I've never had cause to regret.

No one was more surprised than I to learn that Chris Rossiter had been shot to death. When the Indian returned I'd expected to hear of the runner succumbing mysteriously along the trail. Certainly I had put enough laudanum in his morning coffee to do it. I hadn't foreseen the Crow shooting him as he lay helpless, then making up a story about a Cheyenne attack. But I couldn't kill him as he was running away, not from a crime I shared. I credit my later success as an attorney to this same sense of justice.

THE PILGRIM

AUTHOR'S NOTE: "The Pilgrim" is the original opening chapter of The Wolfer, which was published in a different incarnation by Pocket Books in 1981 after a bitter argument with an editor at Doubleday who objected to such 19th-century trappings as lengthy chapter headings and the narrator's formalized language. Those same objections were raised by the editor at Pocket Books, but in a more polite and professional manner, and so I rewrote the book in conventional third person and without chapter headings. The editor who used a few artistic differences to vent all the vitriol of four years' association left Doubleday shortly thereafter to condense books for the Reader's Digest; a fitting punishment, I always thought. His pettiness aside, it's just possible he was right, but I'd prefer to leave it to the reader to decide whether the book would have gained or lost by the original approach.

———

I t has been my great good fortune during my sunset years to have made the acquaintance of former President Theodore Roosevelt, and to consider myself, in spite of our rather savage differences (for no other adjective will suffice) over his attempt to split the Republican Party in 1912, his friend. He it was who suggested I set down the facts attending the brief period I spent with that great frontiersman and forgotten American, Asa North; and should I succumb in my present extremity to the damnable cough which my physicians predicted would claim me thirty years ago before I have had time to prepare a proper dedication, let it be known henceforth that he alone is responsible for the narrative which follows.

Before I proceed, some background is necessary. Having been born in 1846 to a family of scriveners and schoolteachers in Portsmouth, New Hampshire, and graduated from Harvard at a tender age, I was disappointed though not much surprised upon joining the Army of the Potomac in 1865 to find myself a company clerk in Rhode Island. The only action I saw there had to do with a heated correspondence between myself and a quartermaster sergeant at Fort Leavenworth involving a shipment of flannel underwear issued in response to a requisition for twelve cases of new Springfield rifles. Following Lee's surrender, and contrary to the wishes of my parents, who had envisioned me for a career in law, I emigrated to New York City and there applied for and was given a position as reporter on James Gordon Bennett's New York *Herald*. In that assignment I distinguished myself so far as to persuade Bennett's son,

James Gordon, Jr., not to give me the sack when he assumed control of the journal following his father's death in 1872.

I toiled for eleven more years without rising above my original station, and had given up all hope of doing so when I received a telegram from Joseph Pulitzer, founder of the fledgling New York *World,* offering me fresh status as city government reporter with editorial responsibilities at a monthly salary fully twice what I was receiving at the *Herald.* Naturally I accepted, and it was as a Pulitzer employee that I embarked upon the adventure which has inspired this volume.

Lest the reader think my life impossibly barren prior to that winter of 1885, I should add that during my residency in Babylon-upon-the-Hudson I had married and become separated from a young widow from Albany who proved to have the morals but not the discretion of the common alley cat, immersed myself deeply in municipal politics, served two terms as city alderman, and been a delegate to the Republican national convention which nominated Garfield for the presidency in 1880—continuing all the while to discharge my journalistic duties at first one paper and then the other. Along the way I had also contracted a most serious case of emphysema which, threatening to turn into consumption, influenced my decision to seek a healthier climate out West.

The official excuse was a proposed series centered around a number of those colorful characters with which the frontier was said to be filled, but in truth the general interest in things western was not what it had been, and to this day I am convinced that the assignment was little more than a working exile designed to relieve the newsroom of my constant hacking and the fear of exposure to the miasma which was said to surround sufferers of my type of malady. I flatter myself that my ability to transform the Machiavellian concepts of party politics into the most puerile terms for the benefit of our readers was what prevented my editors from discharging me.

I do not know what it was exactly that made me settle upon Rebellion, other than a determination to avoid such picked-over territory as Dodge City and Tombstone. I am fairly certain that I had never heard the name before I booked passage on the Great

Northern Pacific bound to the Northwest, along whose right-of-way lay the last vestiges of the frontier, but by the time I found myself trading the luxury of a Pullman for a seat in a rickety day coach on the Oregon Short Line I had heard enough from those of my fellow passengers who were returning to be convinced that I had stumbled upon an untapped vein of pure gold for the journalist.

My first glimpse of the bonanza was not promising. Huddled between the Caribou and the Big Hole mountains on the twisting thread of water that gives Idaho Territory's Snake River Valley its name, it was a cluster of dark log buildings that looked as if they had started out weary and had long since sunk past despair into tragic resignation.

Directly overhead, a sky the color of mildew hung so low it seemed to cast its shadow over the dull snow upon which the shelters lay scattered as if cast by a gambler's hand. A terrible dread settled over me as I stepped off the platform, bags in hand, into the muddy street—not of death or danger, which would merely have stimulated the creative impulse that had brought me, but rather that I should have to spend the rest of my days amid such cruel boredom.

"Is it always like this?" I asked my traveling companion of the past four hundred miles, a lean old ranch foreman by the name of Dale Crippen, whose great grizzled mustaches appeared by their sheer weight to be dragging his sunbrowned flesh away from the bone beneath. A handful of bearded men in

patched logging jackets were gathered near the platform but made no move to greet any of the trio of
road-weary passengers, all male, that had alighted
with us. I suspected that this was the highlight of
their day.

"Why, hell, no," said the cowhand, around a plug
of tobacco the size of a baby's fist (which I had been
waiting all day for him to expectorate, in vain). "It
will be like this here for a couple of days at the most,
and then things will settle down and get downright
dismal for a while."

His reply took me aback until I glanced at him,
saw a faded blue eye watching me slyly from the
forest of cracks at the corners of his lids, and realized
that I had just been treated to an example of that
famous frontier humor about which I had heard so
much. I countered with the Manhattan equivalent.

"Good. I am in need of rest."

To my surprise, for I had expected the subtlety to
escape him, Crippen winked broadly and served me
a nudge in the ribs with a bony elbow that gave me an
uncomfortable moment lest I subside into a coughing
fit. Thus far in my journey, no one west of Park Row
knew of my real reason for leaving New York, and
that was the way I would have it. By the time I had
mastered myself sufficiently to renew our conversation we had reached the hotel.

This was a square, three-story frame building,
one of only two in town, whose sign running the
length of the front porch identified it as the Assini-

boin Inn. Though it was of fairly recent construction, the paint on one of the porch pillars came off in a grayish dust onto my sleeve when I brushed against it and the iron sconces in which a lantern rested on either side of the door were brown with rust. In general the building was a twin of the structure upon the opposite corner, which sported no sign but which I was to come to know as "Aurora's place," whose frilly curtains concealed the sort of activity one might expect of an establishment popularly referred to, from the nickname of the hotel that faced it, as "the other side of Sin." I remember experiencing a recurrence of the nameless dread as I stepped up onto the booming hotel porch behind Crippen and glimpsed a pair of mannish-looking matrons watching us idly from the balcony of the other building. In the harsh light of day their shimmering dressing gowns and faces splotched with rouge and mascara made me think of corpses shrouded and painted by an inexperienced mortician.

I asked Crippen about the stench that seemed to be coming from the alley which wound behind the Assiniboin. Borne upon the crisp winter air, it was overpowering.

"Skins," he replied. "That's where they tally them before paying out the bounties. This here is the wolfing capital of the Northwest."

The front of the building was something of a town bulletin board, plastered over with posters describing various rustlers and horse thieves and offering inducements to cattlemen to ship stock on the Union Pacific, all but buried beneath scribbled advertisements enumerating various items for sale by local citizens. It was indication enough that the town had no newspaper. One poster in particular caught my eye for the black boldness of the block capitals that made up its top line, reading as follows:

$600 REWARD $600

For the Whole Hide, or other Proof of Death or Capture, of a Black-Mantled Wolf weighing in excess of 100 Pounds, and known as Black Jack, Leader of a Large Pack in the Caribou Foothills whose Depredations among local Herds of Cattle and Wild Game have been the Source of much Concern among the Good Citizens of Rebellion.

$5 BOUNTY $5

For each Wolf Scalp taken in the vicinity of the Snake River Valley, or more than Twice what the Territory of Idaho is offering for the same Item.

Redeemable from any Member of the Idaho Stockmen's Association.

Nelson Meredith, President.

Meredith's signature was a daring indigo slash above the printed name.

"Six hundred dollars seems rather a stiff bounty to pay for a wolf," I commented, indicating the circular.

"Not for this wolf."

Though far from elegant, the lobby of the Assiniboin carried a simple dignity in its sturdy construction and utilitarian furnishings to which no amount of gilt fixtures or burgundy carpeting could add. A broad staircase of hand-rubbed oak led to the upper floors on the other side of a large desk fashioned of the same dark wood, behind which a middle-aged clerk with a round, florid face and blond hair brushed back carefully from a scanty widow's peak stood beaming at us as we entered. He was wearing a black beaver coat in need of brushing and a high starched collar whose exposed seams revealed that it had been freshly turned. When Crippen greeted him I learned that the gentleman's Christian name, unfortunately, was Thanatopsis.

"Is he in?" asked the foreman, after answering a number of questions about his trip to Chicago. He jerked his head in the direction of the stairs.

The clerk nodded. "With the others. He said to send you right up when you arrived."

Crippen started in that direction, leaving behind the worn carpetbag that was his only luggage. "Keep an eye on that. And take good care of my friend here from back East. He knows a joke when he hears one."

"'R. G. Fuiwider,'" read the clerk in his off-key

tenor when I had signed the register. "Is that your full name, sir?"

I assured him that it was and accepted the key to a room on the second floor. There being no bellboy, and the man behind the desk pleading gout, I was carrying my own bags up the complaining staircase when a number of men passed me on their way down. There were eight of them strung out in a line, middle-aged and older, dressed in suits of varying quality under overcoats which seemed a bit heavy for the rather mild temperature outside. Their headgear ranged from derbies not unlike my own, perched at jaunty angles, to the storied "ten-gallon" Stetson, which had proved rarer among the wide open spaces than I had been led to believe. Their faces were either very dark or very pale, with no gradations in between, and there was not a clean-shaven lip among them. To a man they moved with that air of being late for an important appointment elsewhere which I had so often noted in financiers on their way to and from the stock exchange.

Dale Crippen was on my floor speaking with a man who stood in an open doorway with his back to a room full of chairs upholstered in black leather. The stranger was stocky and solid-looking, with a square face admirably suited for his sidewhiskers and a head of thick, wavy auburn hair going silver at the temples. His complexion was hickory brown, fading out as it climbed the planes and hollows of his face and ending in a creamy swath across his forehead where the broad gray brim of the hat he held in one hand would have prevented the sun from reaching. His suit was cut western style, his high boots tilted forward upon two-inch heels and hand-tooled in the Mexican manner, but I suspected that nothing like them was available in town, or anywhere else west of New Bond Street.

Seeing my approach, the foreman broke off the conversation to introduce us. Nelson Meredith regarded me with eyes the shade of blue one sees at the very edge of a tempered blade after a professional sharpener has finished with it, and which flees almost in the time it takes to put it away. It hurt to look at them.

"I hope you will enjoy your stay in my Idaho," he said, offering his hand. I set down a bag to accept it. His grip was like his speech, controlled strength in a guise of softness. He had an English accent. Had I not been told his name, I think I would still have connected him with that bold signature I had seen on the bounty notice downstairs. I guessed our ages to be about the same.

I responded to his welcome with an inanity which escapes me now, and explained the official reason for my trip. He laughed softly, a low, silken rumble that barely stirred the lines of his face.

"I fear that you will be disappointed," he said. "The sort of creature you are hunting no longer exists out here, if indeed he ever did. There is but one Wild Bill Hickok to a century."

"But I am not searching for a Hickok, necessarily. I am certain that our readers back East would be just as eager to learn about big ranchers such as yourself."

"Perhaps, but I am hardly a typical example. My father came to this territory when it was populated only by red Indians and herds of buffalo to whom his title of Knight of the Realm meant nothing. He carved out an empire larger than some European kingdoms with his bare hands and a little help from Mr. Colt. He would have been worth writing about. I was educated at Cambridge and only came out here ten years ago upon my father's death." He smiled without showing his teeth. "I am something of a carpetbagger, you see."

"And the others?"

"You passed some of them on the stairs just now. What is your impression?"

I told him of the comparison I had made with financiers back home. He nodded. "An apt analogy. They are speculators, mainly, from Europe and else-where, who purchased their holdings from men like my father and expanded them by homesteading the sources of water. Which is an illegal practice, though hardly heroic. If it is stories of adventure you want, Dale Crippen is your man. He has brought more cattle up from Texas than the city of Chicago could consume in a decade, and has fought red Indians and outlaws to do it. Unfortunately, his experiences do not greatly differ from those of hundreds of others whose stories have already been repeated for print. I fear that you could merely be covering old ground."

"You paint a bleak picture," said I.

He shrugged, a minimal movement involving but one shoulder. "I am using what colors are available."

"I should like to visit your ranch sometime."

"Dale and I will be returning in the morning. If you would care to accompany us you will be most welcome."

My lungs were beginning to close up. I replied hastily that I would very much like to accompany them, agreed to meet them in Meredith's suite at dawn, and took my leave. I barely got to my room with my luggage when the awful racking began.

When it was done I sat down weakly on the edge of the bed and inspected my handkerchief closely. There was no blood yet. Unstrapping my portmanteau, I excavated a quart bottle of gin from among my shirts, uncorked it, and without bothering to search for a glass tipped it up to dissolve the phlegm which had accumulated in my throat. It worked admirably well. My problem was that I did not stop once it had accomplished its purpose.

THE PIONEER STRAIN

"A rifle!" Vernon Thickett stared up at his fellow deputy from behind a steaming hot bowl of Maud Baxter's notorious Red River Chili and cursed.

Earl Briggs nodded. He was a lean country boy, leaner even than Thickett, and with his shock of unruly wheat-colored hair and freckle-spattered face he looked far too young to be wearing a star on his buff shirt. "That's what I said, Verne," he affirmed. "She's got a rifle and Lord knows how many cartridges up there and she threatened to blow a hole in her nephew's tailormade suit if he didn't clear off her land."

"Did he take her advice?"

A quick grin flashed across the younger deputy's face. "You know Leroy, Verne.

"What do you think?"

"I think he took her advice. Where is he now?"

"Out on Route Forty-four. He called the office from one of those free telephones the Highway Department put in last spring."

"Madder'n a half-squashed bee, I expect." Thicken made a face at his untouched meal and pushed himself reluctantly to his feet. He towered over Earl by a full head. "Get in touch with Luke and Dan and tell 'em to get over to Molly's place on the double and wait for me. No sirens—we don't want any state troopers in on this one. Then bring my car around in front of the office while I grab a gun. That's the only thing the old girl understands." When Earl had left to carry out his orders, Thicken snatched a slice of bread from the table, spooned a quantity of chili onto it, slapped another slice on top of that, and, nodding to hefty Maud Baxter behind the counter, strode toward the door of the diner with the sand-wich in his mouth.

He didn't say a word to Earl all the way out to Molly's place. Verne Thicken was not the law in Schuylerville, Oklahoma, but as long as Sheriff Willis was in the hospital recuperating from a gallbladder operation he was the next best thing. Until now his biggest headache had been the kids who kept stealing the outhouse from behind Guy Dawson's place and hauling it up onto the roof of whatever schoolteacher happened to be the target of their hostilities that week. As for Molly Dodd, she was trouble enough at any time, but the kind of trouble she usually caused seldom involved the law. Molly Dodd armed with a rifle was one problem he wouldn't wish on his worst enemy.

For the past two years she and her nephew, Leroy Cooper, had been engaged in a bitter legal battle with each other over the ownership of the 160 acres she lived on up in the Osage Hills. The Great Midwestern Bank and Trust Company, of which Leroy was the Schuylerville branch manager, claimed the land in lieu of payment on a loan it had made to Molly's late husband Clyde back in 1969, while she maintained that he had paid it off shortly before his death in 1973. Molly, now in her late seventies, had been part of Schuylerville for so long that most of the town had sided with her throughout the complex legal maneuvering, but that had come to an end three weeks before when the county court of appeals found in favor of the bank and issued an order for Molly Dodd's eviction.

Thicken berated himself for not having antici-pated the present situation. The pioneer strain in Molly was too strong to allow her to give in easily. He remembered the story his father had told him of the time she had come home early from a visit to find the house dark and her best friend's flivver parked in the driveway. Instead of going in and shooting Clyde and his lover—which, according to the moral code of the time, would have seemed the natural thing to do—she had simply climbed into the shiny new car, driven it into the next country, and sold it. The story had it that Clyde ended the affair soon afterward, and there was no record in the sheriff's office of a car being stolen that year. True or not, the account was worthy of Molly's reputation for audacity and ingenuity. It was certainly a funnier story than the desperate one currently unfolding up in the hills.

Leroy Cooper's sedan was parked at the side of the private road that led to the house at the top of the hill. A pair of scout cars were parked across from it at different angles. Earl ground the car to a dusty halt behind the civilian vehicle and they got out. Cooper separated himself from the two deputies with whom he had been conversing and came forward. "I want the woman arrested, Deputy!" he exclaimed shrilly. "Do you know she actually threatened to shoot me? I barely got out of there with my life!"

"Take it easy, Leroy." Thicken slid his Stetson to the back of his head with a casual movement of his right hand. "Do you mind telling me what you were doing up there in the first place?"

"I merely reminded her to vacate the premises before midnight tonight. That's the deadline set by the court. The bulldozers come in tomorrow."

"That's our job, Leroy. Why didn't you call us first?"

The banker looked as if Thicken had just asked him to scrub out a spittoon with his monogrammed shirt. "This is a family matter, Deputy. There seemed no reason to involve the law."

"It's a little late for that isn't it—What've we got, Luke?"

Luke Madden, the older of the two deputies already on the scene, was a big man with a bulldog jaw and hair the color of dull steel. He had been a deputy when Wilbur Underhill stormed through the area in 1933, and his prized possession was a framed newspaper clipping which described his inconclusive shoot-out with the outlaw.

He spoke with a Blue Diamond matchstick clamped between his teeth. "That cabin's bunted smack up against the side of the hill," he told Thickett. "There's only one way in or out by car, and this here's it. If you and Earl and Dan can keep her busy in front, Verne, I can sneak around the long way and take her from behind."

"How are you going to get in? Through the chimney?" The chief deputy squinted up at the gabled structure atop the hill. "I reckon we'll just go on up and give her the chance to surrender."

The four-car caravan took off with Earl and Thicken in the lead and Leroy Cooper timidly bringing up the rear in his gleaming sedan. They were rounding the final turn before the house when a shot rang out and a bullet starred the windshield between the two deputies in front. Earl yanked the wheel hard to the right. The unmarked cruiser jumped the bank and came to a jarring stop in a bed of weeds at the side of the road.

They both spilled out Thickett's side of the car

and crouched there, guns drawn. "Verne! Earl! You guys all right?" The voice was Luke Madden's, shouting from behind his car parked perpendicularly across the road. The way beyond it was completely blocked by the other two vehicles.

"We're fine!" Thickett shouted back. "Stay down!"

"She means business," said Earl. "Maybe I ought to radio the state troopers."

"No need. If Molly had meant to hit us, she would have hit us. I've seen her pick nails *off* a fence post at thirty yards. She's just trying to scare us."

"She's awful good at it."

No more shots accompanied the first one, and for a long time the only sound was that of an occasional breeze humming through the upper branches of the towering pines that surrounded the house on three sides. The dwelling itself appeared deserted. All but one of the tall front windows were shaded, the exception being the wide open one to the left of the front door. Five full minutes passed before a voice like a bull's bellow came out through the open window.

"You boys just get back into your automobiles and drive on out of here," it said. "I don't want to hurt nobody, but I will if I have to!"

Cupping his hands around his mouth, Thickett shouted: "Molly, this here's Vernon Thickett! Put down that rifle and let us come in! You're not a criminal! Don't act like one!"

There was a short silence. Then, from the house:

"I've knowed you since you was a baby, Vernon, and you know I don't want to hurt you! But you know I will if it means keepin' what's mine!"

"That's what I want to talk to you about, Molly! I —" Vernon had started to rise when another shot sounded, the bullet zinging along the roof of the unmarked scout car, missing his right ear by a couple of inches. He dove to the ground. "I can see this is going to take more than just words," he said to Earl after a moment.

A series of six more reports followed in rapid succession, and Thicken turned his head as Luke Madden ran toward him in a crouch, bullets kicking up dirt at his heels. "Luke, what in *hell* do you think you're doing?" he demanded when the older deputy was sprawled beside him, panting heavily. "I thought I told you to stay put!"

"Look," said the other, once he'd caught his breath. "If I can get around to the other side of the hill without her seeing me, I can drop down onto the roof and climb in through one of those gabled windows. With you laying down a steady pattern of fire out here she won't suspect a thing until I grab her and take away her rifle."

"No! There's no telling what she'll do if you startle her! Go back. I'll call you when I need you."

"Verne—"

"You heard me! Get back there and help Dan keep an eye on Leroy in case he tries anything dumb."

The other muttered something unintelligible and sprinted back to his car as more shots sounded from the house.

Earl turned a pair of frank blue eyes on Verne. "He might be right, you know. That may be the only way to get her out of there without bloodshed."

"Forget it," snapped Thickett. "The trouble with Luke Madden is he can't forget he's the one who almost got Wilbur Underhill. I'm not going to let him play hero at the expense of that frightened old woman."

"Have you got a better plan?"

Thickett thought. Suddenly he turned to his companion. "What's the name of that salesman from Tulsa, the one who retired and came here to live about five years ago? You know, the one Molly's sweet on?"

"Luther Briscoe?"

"Right. Ever since Clyde's death nobody's seen 'em apart, not even when she went to court. They do everything together. There's that telephone down by the highway; get hold of him and see if you can get him up here. If anybody can talk her out of there, Briscoe can."

"I can't."

"Why not?"

"He left town yesterday to visit his sister in Kansas. He asked me to keep an eye on his house while he was gone. Said he wouldn't be back until Monday."

"Damn! Well, that just leaves Plan B." Thicken jammed his pistol into its holster and began unbuckling the belt.

"What are you doing?"

"I'm going in." He laid the gun belt on the ground.

"You're *what?*"

"I'm counting on our friendship to keep her from shooting me."

"*Now* who's playing hero? You can't be sure of—"

"Hold your fire, Molly!" Thicken shouted through cupped hands. "I'm coming in and I'm unarmed!"

"Don't, Vernon!" The answering bellow held a desperate edge. "I mean what I say! I'll scatter your brains all over these hills!"

"I don't think you will, Molly." Slowly he rose to his feet. A bullet spranged against the roof of the scout car.

Thickett signaled the other deputies to hold their fire and stepped clear of the car. He could see Molly's rifle barrel pointing through the window. Cautiously he took a step forward.

The second shot snatched his hat off his head. He hesitated, then moved on. A third slug whined past his left ear but he kept walking. The next three shots were snapped off so rapidly they sounded as if they had come from a machine-gun. They struck the ground at his feet and spat gravel onto his pant legs. By this time he was almost to the door. Two more steps and he was inside, where he closed the door behind him.

It was a moment before his eyes adjusted themselves to the dim light inside the house. When they had, his first thought was that the interior had not changed since he was a boy. The Victorian clutter, from the overstuffed rockers festooned with doilies to the glass-fronted china cabinets and paper walls upon which hung framed and faded prints of every conceivable shape and size, was the same as he remembered it.

The only difference was the pile of cartridges on the pedestal table beside the door. Beyond it, Molly Dodd stood in the shadows at the open front window, her dark eyes glittering above the stock of the 30-year-old carbine she held braced against her shoulder. Thicken was looking right down its bore.

"Say your piece and get out." Her voice was taut. Small but wiry, she wore her black hair pulled straight back into a tight bun. Although her eyes were small above her hooked nose, they had a remarkable depth of expression. Her mouth was wide and turned down at the corners in a permanent scowl. Her print dress looked new, as did the sweater she wore buttoned at the neck like a cape. The firearm remained steady in her hands.

"Why don't you give me the gun, Molly?" Verne asked quietly. "You aren't going to shoot anyone."

"When it comes to protectin' my property I'd shoot my own son if I had one," she snapped.

"You want to tell me about it?"

There was an almost indiscernible change in the expression of her eyes. "This place is mine," she said. "I know what the courts said, but they was wrong. They didn't see the record that proved Clyde paid off that loan because it don't exist no more. Not after that slippery nephew of mine got rid of it.

"Why would Leroy do that?" Thickett began to breathe a little more easily. He had her talking now.

"Why do you think? He knows there's oil on this land just like everybody else. If he can grab it for his bank he'll make hisself a big man and maybe they'll forget about checkin' his books like they been threatened.

"His books?"

She nodded curtly. Her eyes were black diamonds behind the peep-sight of the rifle. "He's been stealin' money from his accounts for years. You seen that car he drives, the clothes he wears. He can't afford them on his salary. I was in the bank once and overheard a man threatenin' to take his books to the main branch in Oklahoma City to have 'em checked out. Leroy fell all over hisself tryin' to talk him out of it."

Thickett found himself growing interested in spite of the situation. "You say he destroyed the record that proved Clyde repaid the loan? Don't you have any proof of your own? What about a receipt?"

"Clyde never told me what he done with it. I been all over the house. It ain't here."

"What did you hope to gain by barricading yourself in the house?"

She smiled then, a bitter upturn of her cracked and pleated lips. "I wanted to see that squirrel's face when I stuck this here carbine under his nose. I never meant to drag you boys into it, Vernon."

"Don't you think it's gone far enough? Come on, Molly. We're old friends. Give me the piece."

She hesitated. Slowly the hard glitter faded from her eyes. Now she was just a tired old woman. At length she lowered the rifle and handed it to him.

Now that the danger was over, the deputy felt no triumph. For a long moment he regarded Molly with compassionate eyes. "What are your plans?" he asked.

"I sent my luggage on to Mexico this morning."

Mexico? Why Mexico?"

"That's where Clyde and me spent our honeymoon. I got a reservation on a plane leavin' tonight from Tulsa. Don't suppose I'll make it now."

"Not if Leroy decides to press charges."

"That squirrel? Don't worry, he won't do nothin' that might attract the wrong kind of attention." She looked at him apologetically. "I sure am sorry about that busted windshield."

He laughed good-naturedly. "You're good for it, Molly. Besides, the experience was almost worth it." There was an embarrassed silence. Then: "What about Luther Briscoe? What was he going to think when he got back from Kansas and found you gone?"

"That's his business, I expect."

Thickett chose not to press the point. "Well," he drawled, "I'm faced with a decision. I can either put you in jail or drive you into Tulsa in time to catch your plane. Since my duty is to the citizens of Schuylerville, I think I'd be acting in their best interests if I saved them the expense of your room and board and took you into Tulsa."

She placed an affectionate hand on his arm. "You're a good boy, Vernon. I always said that."

It was dusk when Thicken eased the scout car he had borrowed from Luke Madden into the parking slot in front of the sheriff's office and went in. After the long drive back from Tulsa, it felt good to be using his legs again.

Earl Briggs, on his feet behind Thickett's desk, was hanging up the telephone as the chief deputy entered.

"I'm glad you're still here, Earl," Thicken said. "First thing tomorrow morning I want you to get in touch with the Great Midwestern Bank and Trust Company in Oklahoma City and—what is it?"

The look on the boy's face sent a wave of electricity through Thickett's weary limbs. "That was Leroy Cooper," said Earl, inclining his head toward the telephone. "He just got back to find his head cashier tied up and gagged and the rest of his employees locked in the vault. Seems the bank was held up for a quarter of a million dollars while we were all out at Molly's place. You'll never guess who he says did it."

Thicken felt a sinking sensation as the pieces fell into place. He tightened his grip on the doorknob. "Luther Briscoe."

Earl stared at him. "How on earth did you know that?" he said.

YOUNG MISTER ST. JOHN

S t. John learned later that the man he killed was named Jack LeFever. He was a great muddy mixture of dead tribes and an eighth white, with scars like woodworms on his flat broken face and long black greasy curls that hung so far down his back a man couldn't tell where the hair left off and his buffalo coat started. He slapped a filthy coin down on the plank bar and called for whiskey in a voice that creaked like a gallows in the wind.

St. John left the coin on the bar. The only light in the store slid in through a grease-paper window over a stack of green hides and glowered on the dull token. St. John said, "Whiskey here's a quarter."

"Pour it."

"That there's a nickel."

"It's a quarter."

"Look for yourself."

The breed's rheumy eyes never left St. John's face. "If it's a nickel, you switched coins."

"I never touched it."

"You're a liar."

St. John squeezed the trigger of the sawed-off under the bar. The charge lifted the breed off his feet and hurled him back against the pine post that held up the roof, hard enough to crack it and bring down a hatful of dirt and dead spiders from the ceiling.

The pale scars disappeared against his blanched, surprised face and he slid into a sitting position in the blood and excrement on the dirt floor.

"Told you it was a nickel," St. John said.

The roar had swallowed up all the lesser sounds, and through the slowly curling blue smoke walked a big man with large, cracked, oddly Oriental features, two points of a nickel-plated star showing under his corduroy coat. He was pointing a Navy Colt's at St. John.

The bartender had used up both barrels on the breed. He reached for his Peacemaker in its holster under the bar, but the lawman was faster. The Navy's barrel split the flesh on St. John's cheek and he fell among the kegs of molasses against the back wall. The big man leaned across the bar and scooped out the Peacemaker.

"I was fixing to arrest you for selling whiskey in the Nations," he said. "I reckon Judge Parker will settle for murder. On your feet."

He was taken in shackles across the Arkansas

border into Fort Smith, a cluster of dowdy military blockhouses enclosed by a stockade whose gate had stood open ever since the last soldier had left. The only feature of interest was the gallows behind the stone commissary building. It was twenty feet long with an I-beam twelve inches thick to suspend the nooses from when in use. The lawman, whose name was Amos, noted St. John's interest.

"It will hold your likes right enough, and eleven more. Parker does like to save 'em up."

A flight of wooden steps led from the two-story brick courthouse to a basement containing two cells, each twenty-nine by fifty-five feet (St. John paced his off many times in the succeeding weeks) and separated by a solid stone wall. The prisoner sat on a floor slimy with lichens among six other men who didn't talk and urinated and defecated into a bucket kept in the cold chimney. On bath days he crouched in a kerosene barrel cut in half and scrubbed himself with cold water and gritty yellow soap. Because it was always night in the basement, he told time by counting baths. One bath every ten days, three to a month. After four baths a guard came for him.

The unaccustomed exercise, together with the weight of his leg irons, set his leg muscles aching during the climb upstairs. The guard knocked on a dark oak door in a quiet hallway and opened it and pushed him inside.

"Prisoner St. John, your honor."

St. John blinked in the sunlight coming through

the windows. The man seated behind the big desk looked at him with heavy-lidded eyes the way a stock trader looked at meat on the hoof. He had calm brows and carefully brushed dark hair growing gray at the part and a wiry goatee and neat mustache, also graying; but for all that he was a comparatively young man, thirty-five at the outside. He wore a black suit and waistcoat with a gold watch chain and a maroon silk tie.

"Remove his shackles."

The guard's key grated. St. John resisted the temptation to rub his wrists and ankles. The man dismissed the guard, who hesitated.

"It's all right," said the man behind the desk. "Mr. McAdoo is here."

The guard left. St. John noticed the other party for the first time, standing by the shelves of mustard-colored books opposite the desk. He was thickset and wore a great handlebar and too-tight three-piece suit and looked some years older than the seated man.

"Do you know who I am?" asked the man behind the desk.

St. John worked his tongue. "You're Parker. I seen your picture once in a whorehouse in the Cherokee Strip. It had six bullet holes in it."

"*Judge* Parker." McAdoo glared over his handlebars.

"Forgive the formality," said Judge Parker. "Fort Smith is a new court and we're proud of our titles. Mr. McAdoo is United States Marshal for this district. And you are Irons St. John, murderer. The same Irons St. John tried in Austin last year for robbing the Texas and Pacific Railroad."

"The jury turned me loose."

"The prosecution was pathetic. I've studied the case. There is, however, no question about the verdict this time. Deputy Ames saw you slay Jack LeFever in cold blood."

"Breeds don't bleed cold. And he called me a liar."

"Is that a capital offense where you come from?"

"I don't call any man liar unless I know it, and I require the same."

Parker rested his forearms on the desk. "There is only one penalty for willful murder under the law, and no appeal between this bench and almighty God. How old are you?"

"Twenty."

"I cannot think of a greater crime than to die at twenty." The sorrow in the heavy- lidded eyes looked real.

"Ain't that up to the jury?"

"The jury will continue to discharge its duty as it has since I took this assignment. However." He paused. "There are special circumstances in this case, which I may or may not rule pertinent according to my lights. LeFever was wanted for rape and murder. Had you not met, he would likely have been appre-hended and hanged by Easter."

"Christmas, maybe," said St. John.

The judge ignored the comment. "Mark you, this is not license for just anyone to run out and do the law's work. But such facts have been known to sway jurors."

"Spit out what you're chewing on. Your honor."

Parker sat back and gripped the padded leather arms of his chair. "Last year, the Congress granted this court criminal jurisdiction over the Indian Nations, and a mere two hundred deputy marshals to patrol seventy-four thousand square miles of wilderness. This job requires unpleasant men. Wouldn't you agree, Mr. McAdoo?"

"Juggers and cornholers, the lot of them."

"Precisely. I daresay more than a few have been fitted for nooses somewhere."

St. John was beginning to get the idea. He looked at McAdoo. "Can he do that?"

"Till the Congress says stop," said the marshal. "And they ain't said it yet."

"Mr. McAdoo has more badges than chests to pin them on," Judge Parker said. "The star or the rope, St. John. Which will you have?"

"I'll be damned."

"I will allow no profanity in this court. You haven't answered my question."

"What's it pay?"

Judge Parker may have smiled; St. John couldn't be sure. "Really, does it matter?"

"I reckon not," said St. John, and went to work for the government.

A WEB OF BOOKS

The visitor stepped inside the bookshop and blinked. The muted light and cool, dank air seemed otherworldly after the bright heat of the New Mexico street. As he closed the door, feathers of dust clinging to the spines of the decaying volumes on the shelves crawled and twitched in the current air. The place smelled of must.

"Can I help you?" bleated the old man seated behind the dented desk. He was thin and angular, his shoulders falling away under a fraying sweater. Dull black hair spilled untidily over his collar. His face was narrow and puckered and dominated by spectacles so thick he seemed to be peering from the other side of a fish tank.

"Are you the owner?"

The old man nodded. "My name is Sharecross."

"Jed Kirby. I'm an investigator with Southwestern Life and Property." He didn't offer to shake hands. The missing finger on his right hand, a souvenir of Korea, provoked questions he was tired of answering. "I tried to call you yesterday."

"The lines are down east of town. A Santa Ana blew through over the weekend." Kirby dismissed it with a wave of his good hand. "I'm looking for a man named Murchison, Alan Murchison. We think he has information about an item of missing property insured by us."

"I don't know the name. Is it a book that's missing?"

"A very rare volume entitled *The Midnight Sky*, by James Edward Long, published in Edinburgh in 1758. About ten inches by seven, four hundred and fifty pages, bound in brown morocco with gold leaf on the page ends. It was stolen from a private library in Albuquerque last month. We think Murchison is the thief."

"Ah, that one," Sharecross said. "Only two copies are known to exist. Each is worth as much as some whole collections. What makes you think he'd come here?"

"He's on the run. He was nearly apprehended in Silver City, but he managed to elude the police. He'll probably try to unload the book for whatever he can get and use the money to skip to South America. Our information has him heading this way."

"Dear me, that seems like a lot of trouble over one book, even The Midnight Sky."

"The book's just part of it, although it's the part

that most directly concerns us. The law would dearly love to have him. He murdered the owner in order to gain possession."

"Dear me," repeated the bookseller.

"It pieces together like this." Kirby caught himself gesturing with the incomplete hand and switched. "Murchison, a dealer who supplies rare curiosities to collectors who don't ask questions, went to this man Scullock with an offer to buy the book. When Scullock refused to sell, Murchison lost control and split the fellow's cranium with a bronze bust of Homer the police found near the body. Then he grabbed the book and left. When his customer got suspicious and backed out of the deal, he took off."

Sharecross looked thoughtful. "Your company must be particularly anxious to recover the item, since you beat the police here."

"It's insured for two hundred thousand dollars, payable to Scullock's heirs if we fail to get it back. My employers aren't in business for their health."

"Who is?" The old man stretched a scrawny arm and lifted a book the size and thickness of a bathroom tile from a stack at his feet. "Two hundred thousand is far outside my budget, Mr. Kirby. This is more my speed." He handed it to the visitor.

It was bound in burgundy leather, heavier than it looked. Kirby ran fingers over the handtooling, opened it carefully, and glanced at the publisher's ads bound into the back of the book. "First edition?"

"Third. Browning's Ring and the Book, the one

with the erratum on page seventy- seven. I paid seven hundred and fifty dollars for it in Las Cruces two years ago. That's more than I can afford to pay for any book, but I couldn't resist it. The pension I get from the Santa Fe Police Department won't stand that kind of strain often."

Kirby looked up, startled. "You were a policeman?"

"Detective. Many years ago, I'm afraid."

Too many, thought the other. He returned the book. "Old books don't really interest me. You'd know Murchison if you saw him. He's small, kind of fragile-looking, with prematurely white hair. Wears tweed jackets and smokes a pipe."

A fresh furrow appeared in Sharecross's forehead. "He's been in, hasn't he?"

"Just once." The old man fondled the Browning. "To buy a book, not sell one. A badly dilapidated copy of Shakespeare's tragedies for ten dollars. That was yesterday. He said his name was Thacker. I think he's staying at the hotel."

"Where's that?"

"Across the street, next to the old town well."

Kirby hurried out. As the door closed behind him he glimpsed Sharecross easing a thick volume down from a high shelf.

Twenty minutes later the visitor was back. Behind the desk Sharecross lifted his eyebrows inquisitively over the big book. It was a current volume of *Who's Who in Book Collecting*.

"What kind of law you got around here?" Kirby demanded.

"Sheriff McCreedy," came the reply after a moment. "But he's at the county seat. There's no way to reach him with the telephone lines down, short of going there. What's wrong?"

"Murchison's dead. Someone shot him."

"Shot him! Are you sure?"

"Bullets make holes. The blood's still fresh." Kirby paused. "The book isn't in his room. I searched." Sharecross dragged over the old-fashioned upright telephone on his desk. "You said the lines were down," Kirby reminded him.

"Not in town. Hello, Birdie?" He spoke into the mouthpiece. "Birdie, get hold of Uncle Ned and ask him to fetch the sheriff. It's urgent." He rang off. To Kirby:

"Ned Scoffield's ninety-seven, but he can make that old Indian motorcycle of his sing. He'll have the law here by sundown."

"Whoever killed Murchison was after the book. Now that he has it, there's no way he'll be within fifty miles of here by sundown."

"Maybe he doesn't have it. Did you search Murchison's car?"

"Car!" Kirby cuffed his forehead. "Stupid! He didn't walk here. Where would I find it?"

"Behind the hotel would be my guess. That's where all the guests park. Maybe you should wait for the sheriff." But the old man was talking to the visitor's back. He was already out the door.

Kirby got the dead man's license number from an upset clerk at the front desk. The plate belonged to a late-model sedan under a skin of desert dust. The inside was an oven. He stripped off his jacket and got to work. After half an hour he climbed out, empty-handed and gasping, and leaned back against a fender to mop his face with a soaked handkerchief. Sharecross approached through shimmering waves of heat, Who's Who under one arm.

"Nothing?"

Kirby, too overheated to talk, shook his head.

"I see you checked out the trunk and engine compartment," observed the bookseller, nodding at the open lid and dislodged hood. "I just came from Murchison's room. He was shot twice at close range. Whoever did it must have used a silencer or he'd have alerted everyone in the hotel."

"What were you doing there?" Kirby was cooling off slowly. Dusk was gathering. "I conducted a search of my own. Once a cop, always a cop. There's something missing besides *The Midnight Sky*."

"A towel?"

"The Shakespeare I sold him. You didn't happen to find it?"

"No, but why should you care? You got your ten bucks."

"It seems to me a thief who'd kill for Long's *magnum opus* couldn't be bothered with such a common item. Also, I asked some of the other merchants what they could tell me about Thacker, or Murchison, of whatever he was calling himself. Carl Lathrop at the dry goods store said he sold Thacker a thirty-foot extension cord last night just before closing."

The other contemplated his handkerchief. "What would he have wanted with that?"

"That's one mystery. Another is why was he wasting time here when he knew the law and your company were on his heels? Why stop here at all, for that matter? Why not head straight for Mexico and peddle the book in one of the major tourist centers? He seems to have made a lot of mistakes for an experienced criminal."

"He'd never been chased before. Maybe he panicked."

"Maybe," agreed Sharecross. "Or maybe he came here to meet a partner. Maybe it was his partner who killed him. Well, we can stand here spinning theories all night and freeze to death. The desert cools off fast when the sun goes down. Why don't we go back to the shop and wait for the sheriff?"

On the way they passed the town well. It was partially boarded over and the ancient peaked roof leaned ten degrees off plumb.

"If it's dry it should be torn down and the hole filled in," Kirby observed. "It's a safety hazard. Someone could fall in."

"You're probably right, but I'll be sorry to see it

go. When it does I'll be the second oldest thing in town after Uncle Ned Scoffield."

The bookshop seemed even gloomier by electric light. Pacing up and down, glancing at the titles on the shelves, Kirby asked his host why he had quit the police. "Job get too tough?"

"It got too easy. The pattern never varies. Someone commits a crime and attempts to confuse the issue, but the more he tries the simpler it grows. He spins a web and ends up catching himself." He wiped his glasses. His eyes were sardine-colored. "I find tracing a book's provenance far more challenging."

Sirens shattered the desert peace. Two blue and white prowl cars ground to a halt in front of the shop, their lights throbbing and splashing red and blue all over the street. A middle-aged man whose tanned face matched the color of his uniform shirt strode in, towing three deputies in similar attire. They all wore Stetsons and high boots.

"What's going on, Avery?" demanded the man in front.

"Murder, Sheriff." Sharecross put on his spectacles. "The victim is registered at the hotel under the name Thacker, though he's known elsewhere as Alan Murchison. You'll find him in Room 14 with two bullets in his chest." He indicated Kirby. "I think a paraffin test on this gentleman's hands will show within a reasonable margin of certainty that he fired the gun that put them there."

Before Kirby could react, one of the deputies seized him and hurled him up against a wall full of books. He was commanded to brace himself on his arms and spread his feet. "The old man's crazy!" he protested. "What motive would I have to—" Rough hands frisked him.

Sharecross said, "You won't find the gun on him. My guess is he chucked it into the well. As things stood he barely had time to kill Murchison, search his room for the book, ditch the murder weapon, and come back here to report the crime."

Sheriff McCreedy directed his deputies to watch the prisoner and accompanied Sharecross outside. The sun was almost gone.

"I've something else to show you before we look at the body." The old man filled him in on the way to the abandoned well.

"Kirby was the dead man's partner," he explained when the sheriff had been brought up to date. "Or perhaps I should refer to him as Jed Carlisle instead of Kirby. That's the name he's listed under in *Who's Who in Book Collecting*. Carlisle was the customer who commissioned Murchison to find *The Midnight Sky*. The way I read things, Murchison tried to shake him down for more money by threatening to pin the owner's murder on his customer. Carlisle agreed to his terms, said he'd meet him here. It's an out-of-the-way place, perfect for what he had in mind. Then he came here, posing as an insurance investigator to throw off the authorities, and shot Murchison to death. He made two mistakes. The first was failing to find out where the book was hidden before he silenced his victim.

"I don't think Kirby, or Carlisle, has much respect for rural law officers, Sheriff. When a search of Murchison's hotel room and car didn't yield his prize he was content to sit back and let you comb the town for it, confident that when it was found he could step forward and claim it for his 'company.' But then he was more bold than smart or he wouldn't have planned this whole thing the way he did."

The sheriff pulled at his lower lip. "What made you suspect him in the first place?"

"He seemed to have more than an employee's knowledge of that book. I tested him by handing him a rare Browning. He claimed that kind of thing didn't interest him; if that were so he would simply have glanced at it to be polite and handed it back. Instead he stroked the binding, lifted open the cover as if were made of glass, looked closely at the advertisement bound in at the back. After that I consulted Who's Who, going through it entry by entry until I found one that fit the man I knew as Jed Kirby. There aren't very many wealthy bibliophiles who are missing the third finger from their right hand. It's a Carlisle trademark, like J. Pierpont Morgan's swollen nose."

"You said he made two mistakes. What was the second?"

"Look in the well."

Shadows filled the ancient excavation. McCreedy produced his flashlight and switched it on. Sharecross directed him to train the beam up under the dilapidated roof. Near the apex, secured by a black cord to the rod that had once supported the bucket, dangled a thick volume with a worn cover beginning to split along the hinge.

"Is that *The Midnight Sky?*" asked the sheriff.

"Hardly." The bookseller untied the second knot that held the book in place. It dropped into the well, pulling its cord. As it descended, a paper-wrapped parcel roughly the same size rose from the depths. Sharecross freed it from the cord and unwrapped it. The sheriff's flashlight gleamed off handsome leather and gold leaf. "Carlisle's second mistake was being in too much of a hurry when he disposed of the gun. He should have looked at the well more closely. The Shakespeare made the perfect counterweight. Note what Murchison tied them with."

McCreedy examined it. "Looks like an extension cord."

"Thirty feet long, I should judge. It was Murchison's last trick. If he'd purchased that much rope and Carlisle found out, the well would have seemed the logical next step. Extension cord was just offbeat enough to keep everyone guessing."

"Except you."

The old man ignored the reluctant compliment. "I told Carlisle earlier that the criminal often catches himself in his own web. This one was spun out of leather and buckram and gold and paper. A web of books. Murchison used a book to help conceal the book he had committed murder to obtain. That book, and Carlisle's obsession to have it, drove him to murder the murderer. A book made me suspect him, and another book led to his identification and apprehension. And now, sheriff—" he paused, uncomfortably and adjusted his spectacles on his thin nose—"I imagine it's your intention to, er, throw the book at him."

Sheriff McCreedy stared at him in mute accusation.

"Yes. Well," said Sharecross, and turned back in the direction of his shop.

MAGO'S BRIDE

In San Hermoso there was always *fiesta* whenever Mago took a wife.

He had had two that year. One, a plump Castilian, had died during the trek across Chihuahua in August. The other, a dark and glowering *rustica* from one of the anonymous pueblos along the Bravo, had bored Mago before a month was out and been packed off to a convent in Mexico City. No one discussed his first bride, an American girl seized in Las Cruces who flung herself from the bell tower of the San Hermoso church on their wedding night years before; but all remember the three days of *fiesta* that had preceded the ceremony.

So it was that when the Magistas learned of the bandit chief's approach with yet another prospective *señora* in tow, they hauled three long tables of unplaned pine from the cantina into the plaza, loaded them with delicacies liberated from pilgrims, butchered three fat heifers that Don Alberto would never miss from his herd of twenty thousand, and laid the pits with mesquite. Tequila and cerveza were conjured up from hidden stores and Otto von Streubing, Mago's lieutenant and a disgraced Hapsburg prince (or so he styled himself), went out with a party in search of antelope. These preparations were made with great solemnity; for marriage was serious business among the Christ-loving people of San Hermoso, and there was nothing frivolous about the way those who did *not* love Christ took their pleasure.

When the outriders returned to announce Mago, his men and their women gathered at the edge of the plaza to greet him. He was galloping his favorite mount, a glossy black gelding presented by the American President to an officer of Porfirio Daiz and claimed by Mago from between the dying officer's thighs at Veracruz. Riding behind the cantle, fingers laced tightly across the chief's middle to avoid falling, was a woman unknown, with a face dark as teak inside the sable tent of her hair.

"*Yaqui*," muttered the watchers; and those young enough to remember their catechisms crossed themselves, for her soiled blouse and dark skirts were certainly of Indian manufacture.

To Mago, of course, they would say nothing. Hall Yaqui himself, with the black eyes and volcanic temperament of the breed, he had also the long memory for personal wrongs that came with his mother's Spanish blood. Even now he was coming hard as in wrath.

"The church!" he roared—and plunged, horse and rider, into the crowd without stopping.

Those with their wits about them flung themselves aside. Those without fell with broken bones and flesh torn by the gelding's steel-shod hoofs. Mago did not stop for them nor even for the heavy-laden tables in his path, but dug in his heels, and the gelding bounced screaming up and over all three, coming down on the other side with a heaving grunt and clawing for traction on the ground before the church.

Behind him, thunder rolled. Someone—the chief himself, perhaps, for he had continued without dismounting through the great yawning iron-banded doors of the church—swung the bell in the tower, clanging the alarm. Shouting, the Magistas and their women trailed him inside and managed with belated efficiency to draw the doors shut. Desperate fists hammered the bar into place.

The church had been designed as a fort in a land scarce in Christians. By the time the men took up their armed posts at the windows, the myriad heads of the enemy could be seen topping the eastern horizon like a black dawn. Here and there an iron-wood lance swayed against the sky, bearing its inevitable human trophy. The word *Apache* sibilated like telegraph current from window to window.

Mago, mounted still, was alone in the saddle. Of

the woman there was no sign. He swept off his sombrero, allowing his dull black hair to tumble in its two famous locks across his temples, and barked orders in rapid dialect. Otto von Streubing, who comprehended little of it, asked what had happened. Mago smiled down at him.

"How close?" he inquired of the nearest sentry.

"Still outside rifle range, *mi jefe*. They have stopped, I think."

"The bastard thinks too much. It will kill him yet." Swinging down, the bandit chief started up the stone steps to the bell tower, jerking his head for Otto to follow.

At the top of the steep flight, Mago rapped on the low door. The pair were admitted by Juan Griz. Brown-eyed, wavy of hair, and built along the lines of a young cougar, Juan was easily the handsomest of those who followed Mago, as well as the most loyal and doglike. The simplest tasks were his great mission.

On the opposite side of the great iron bell, limned in the open arch by the sun, stood the loveliest woman the German had ever seen. Her hair was as dark as the Black Forest, her figure beneath the travel-stained clothes trim and fragile compared to the thick-waisted squaws he had known during his short time in the New World. Her eyes were wary. She seemed poised to fling herself into space. Otto thought—and immediately discarded the thought—of the fate of Mago's first wife. Instinctively he knew that this one would not make that same choice.

"Handsome baggage," he said finally.

"Your fourth, I think. But what—"

Mago reached out and snatched the fine silver chain that hung around the woman's neck. She flinched, catching herself on the archway. Mago dangled the crucifix before his lieutenant's face.

"I know that piece," said Otto.

"You should, my friend. You have seen it around Nochebueno's neck often enough."

"Lieber Gott! What has she to do with that *verdammt* Christian Indian?"

"Cervata is her name. 'Fawn' in the English you insist on using here instead of good Spanish. I found her bathing in a stream outside Nochebueno's camp. Mind you, had I known how she scratches, I would not have allowed her to dress before we left." He put a hand to the place where blood had dried on his cheek. "It was not until I saw the crucifix that I knew she had until late been scratching that Apache bastard."

"I do not imagine it occurred to you to return her."

"My friend, it is foreign to my nature to return things."

The woman spat a stream of mangled Spanish. The gist if not the words reached the German well enough. "How did you manage to get this far?"

"Fortunately for my eyes, she hates the baptized

savage more than she does me. I, however, am in love."

A Magista with machete scars on both cheeks stormed through the open doorway, shoving aside Juan Griz. *"Mi jefe!* The Apaches are attacking!" A crackle of carbines from outside nearly drowned out the words.

Otto von Streubing was the finest marksman in San Hermoso. Mago stationed him in the tower with his excellent Mauser rifle, ordered Juan Griz to keep Cerveta away from the openings, and accompanied the other Magista downstairs. For the next quarter-hour the bandit chief busied himself with the fortress's defense, directing the men's fire and satisfying himself that the women were supplying them with loaded weapons as needed. The sun had begun to set. As shadows enveloped them, the Apaches withdrew, bearing their dead.

"What are our losses?" demanded Mago of the man with the machete scars. "Two dead, *mi jefe;* Paco Mendolo and the boy Gonzales. Your cousin Manuel has lost an ear."

"Which one?"

"The left, I think."

Otto descended from the tower, where he had managed to pluck three savages off their mounts from three hundred yards. "It is not like Nochebueno to give up so easily," he said.

"A reprieve," said Mago. "It takes more than his Jesus to convince his braves their dead will find their way to the Happy Hunting Ground in the dark. At dawn the sun will be at their backs and in our eyes. Then they will throw everything they have at us."

"Not if we give them the woman tonight."

"I never give."

The bandits were quiet that night. If any of them wondered that their fates were caught up with Mago's marital aspirations, none spoke of it. As for the chief, he had retired to the rectory, which had become his quarters upon the departure of the mission's last padre. Otto entered without knocking and stood an unopened bottle of tequila on the great oak desk behind which his general sat eating rat cheese off the blade of his bowie.

"I confiscated it," the German explained. "I thought you might like some of them sober in the morning."

"*Gracias, amigo.* I shall consider it a wedding gift."

"Who will perform the ceremony this time?"

"That Dominican in Santa Carla has not done me a favor in a year."

"I suppose Manuel will stand up for you as always?"

"Manuel is infirm. I would ask you, but I imagine you are an infidel."

"Lutheran."

"As I said." Mago pulled the cork and tossed it over his shoulder. "Well, they can hardly excommunicate me again. To my best man." He lifted the bottle and drank.

Otto watched a drop trickle down his superior's stubbled chin. "I would take my pleasure now. You may not live to dance at your wedding."

"I do not bed women not my wives."

Someone battered the rectory door. Otto admitted a flat-faced Magista who was more Indian than Mexican and less man than animal, who handed Mago a short-shafted arrow with the head broken *off*. The German could follow little of his speech, but gathered that the arrow had narrowly missed a bandit dozing at a window and buried itself in the oaken altar. Mago untied a square of hide from the shaft and read the words burned into it.

"Curse an Indian who knows his letters," he said mildly. "He wishes to meet with me outside San Hermoso in an hour."

"Nochebueno?" said Otto. "What can he want to talk about?"

"We will know in an hour."

The site chosen was a patch of desert midway between the stronghold and the place where the Apaches had made camp. Nochebueno arrived first astride a blaze-faced sorrel, accompanied by two mounted warriors. Nearly as tall as his late fabled grandfather Mangas Coloradas, he was naked save for breechclout and moccasins and a rosary around his thick neck. His face was painted in halves of black and vermilion and resembled nothing so much as a particolored skull. Mago, who had selected a bay mare while his black gelding rested, halted beyond the light of the torches held by the two braves and turned to Otto.

"The ring on his finger, amigo. Do you see it?"

The German squinted. A large ring of what appeared to be polished silver glittered on the Apache chief's right index finger. "A signal ring?"

"They were wizards with mirrors. You will remain here and fire your wonderful foreign rifle if he raises that hand."

Otto snaked his Mauser from the saddle scabbard. "Pray the torches do not flicker." The bandit leader left him.

"Mago!" Nochebueno bared uncommonly fine teeth for an Indian. His Spanish was purer than the Mexican's. "I have not seen you these three years. You look well."

The other drew rein inside the torchlight. "Never better, Noche. I am preparing to marry."

Although the grin remained in place, something very like malice tautened the flat features beneath the warpaint. "Step down, my friend," said he. "We have business."

"All of us?" Mago's gaze took in the two stony-faced braves at Nochebueno's elbows.

The Apache said something in his native tongue. The braves leaned over, jammed the pointed ends of the torches into the earth, wheeled their mounts, and cantered back the way they had come. The bandit leader and the Indian chief stepped down then and squatted on their heels.

"You have a woman in San Hermoso," Nochebueno began.

"*Amigo,* I have had many women, in and out of San Hermoso."

"This one is a personal favorite, purchased at the expense of several very good horses from her father, who manages a coffee plantation near Chiapas. I would have her back."

Mago showed a gold tooth. "You would have her back, and I would have her stay, and that is how it will be all night and all day tomorrow. I waste my time." But he made no move to rise.

"You waste more than time, my friend. You waste the lives of every man, woman, and child in San Hermoso."

"I hear the lion's roar. I do not see his claws."

Nochebueno reached behind him and produced a knife from a sheath at his waist.

It was of European manufacture, with a long slender Sheffield blade and a heavily worked hilt fashioned after a cross.

"A souvenir from my former days of darkness, stolen from a cathedral in Acapulco," he said. "It dates back to the Crusades."

"Your invitation said no weapons, amigo."

"It did, and you may stop fingering that derringer in your pocket. I have not brought it as a weapon."

Mago waited.

"A game!" barked the Indian suddenly, making the torches waver. "You who know me so well know also my passion for sport. I suggest a contest to settle what would otherwise be a long and bloody fight, most un-Christian. My friend, are you feeling strong this night?"

"What are the rules?"

"My question is answered." With a sudden movement, Nochebueno sank the knife to its hilt in the hard earth between them. The shaft threw a shadow in the shape of a crucifix. "We shall he upon our stomachs facing each other, each with a hand on the handle of the knife. If you are the first to snap the blade, the woman is yours, and my warriors and I shall ride from this place in peace."

"And if you are first?"

"My friend, that is entirely up to you. Naturally, I would prefer if in the spirit of sport you would surrender the woman, in which case we would ride from this place in peace. Women, they are for pleasure, not war."

"And yet you are prepared to make war if I refuse this contest."

The Indian's grin was diabolical. "You will not refuse. I see in your eyes that you will not. Am I wrong?"

In response, the bandit chief stretched out on his stomach and grasped the handle. "So it is; so it has always been," said Nochebueno, assuming the same position, fingers interlaced with Mago's. *El Indio y el conquistador*. To the end."

The Mexican was born strong and hardened from the saddle; the Apache, smaller and built along slighter lines, was as a hot wind with meanness and hatred for Mago and all his kind. Their hands quivered and grew slick with sweat. The torches burned low.

There was an ear-splitting snap. Roaring triumphantly, Mago sprang to his knees waving the handle with its broken piece of blade.

"Congratulations, my friend." Nochebueno gathered his legs beneath him. His right hand shot up. It had no index finger.

As he gaped at the bleeding stump, the crack of Otto von Streubing's Mauser rifle reached the place where the two men kneeled. The bullet had taken away finger and signal ring in one pass.

With a savage cry the Apache chief was on his feet, followed by Mago, clawing for the derringer in his pocket. Before the watching braves could react, Otto galloped between the pair. He threw the bay mare's reins to Mango, who vaulted into the saddle and swung toward San Hermoso just as the Apaches began *firing*. The bay mare screamed and *fell*. Mago landed on his feet, caught hold of the German's outstretched hand, and riding double the bandits fled through a hail of fire in the direction of the strong-hold. Behind them Nochebueno shrieked Christian obscenities in Spanish and shook his bloody fist, unwittingly spoiling his brave's aim.

"Fine shooting, *amigo*," Mago shouted over the hammering hooves.

"Not so fine," said the other sourly. "I was aiming for his throat."

The Magista with the machete scars opened the church door for them. Otto handed him his horse's reins. "Wake the others and tell them to prepare for siege," he said.

Mago said, "Let them sleep. The bastards will not attack before morning, if then. If I know Nochebueno, he is hallway back to his village, squawling for the medicine man to wrap his finger. Whatever bowels his people's god gave him he surrendered when he accepted Christ. Close the door, *amigo*. Why do you stand there?"

The Magista was peering into the darkness of the plaza. "Did not the others return with you, *jefe?*"

"What others?"

"Juan Griz and the Yaqui woman. He said you had left orders to join you with the woman and your black gelding. He sent me for his piebald."

Mago said a thing not properly spoke in church and charged up the stone steps to the bell tower, taking them two at a time. Otto seized the man's collar. "When?"

"Just after you and *el jefe* left, *senor*. Juan said—"

"Juan Griz never said a thing in his life not placed in his mouth by someone smarter. I knew this woman was a witch when I first laid eyes on her."

Mago came down as swiftly as he had gone up. He was buckling on a cartridge belt. "Fresh mounts, Otto, quickly! They cannot have gotten far in this darkness."

"There is no catching that gelding when it is rested. If we capture anyone, it will be Juan."

"Then I will have his testicles! Why do you laugh, *amigo?*"

Otto was astonished to find that he was, indeed, laughing. He had not done so since coming to this barbaric place where Christians fought Christians and men stabled their horses in church.

"I laugh because it is funny, Mago. Do you not see how funny it is? While you and Nochebueno were fighting like knights for Cerveta's fine brown hand, Juan Griz was absconding with the rest of her. Not to mention your favorite mount. Or do I mix the two?" He was becoming silly in his mirth. It had spread to the scarred Magista, who cast frightened eyes upon his chief at first, then forgot him in his own helplessness.

Mago scowled. Madness had entered his camp. And then he, too, began to laugh. It was either that or slay two of his best men.

"Well," said he, when they had begun to master themselves, "of what worth is a bride who chooses pleasing looks over intelligence and courage? Wake the men, Otto! We have won one victory this night, and a woman is a small price to pay for Nochebueno's finger."

That night, San Hermoso rang with the din *of fiesta*.

BAD BLOOD

Light spread gray through the sycamores, igniting billions of hanging droplets with the black trunks standing among them looking not fixed to the earth but suspended from above like stalactites. A mockingbird awoke to release its complex scan into the sopping air. There was no answer and the song was not repeated. Leaves crackled, drying.

The man was already awake, a tense silhouette against a yellowing sun louvered by vertical tree shafts, a knee on the ground, the other drawn up to his chest and one fist wrapped around a rifle with its butt planted in the moist earth. His profile was sharp, with a pointed nose like a check mark, the angle dramatized by a long stiff bill tilting down from a green cap with JOHN DEERE embossed in block letters on a patch on the front of the crown. His shirt was coarse and blue under a red and black checked jacket with darns on the elbows. His jeans had been blue but were now earth-colored, like his boots under their cake of silver clay. He had been there in that position since an hour before dawn.

From where he was crouched, the ground fell off forty-five degrees to a berry thicket that girdled the mountain. The thicket had been transplanted by his great-grandfather from a nearby bog and allowed to grow wild until it resembled the tangled barbed wire in which the great-grandfather's son would snare himself thirty years later and wait for the sun to rise and the Germans to discover him in a muddy place called Ypres. This natural barrier had trapped a number of local men the same way, to wait like the soldier and, now, like the soldier's grandson for the dawn and what the dawn would bring.

The slope bristled with leafed trees and cedars and twisted jackpines, heirs to the great towering monarchs that had fallen to the timber boom of another century, whose black stumps still dotted the mountainside like rotted teeth.

A third of the way down the slope, a hundred feet below him and two hundred feet above the thicket, stood his own shack. It had been built of logs when James Monroe was president, but a later ancestor had nailed clapboard over the logs to make it resemble a proper house. A four-paned window that had been covered with oiled paper before the coming of the railroad now reflected sunlight from three panes,

emphasizing the blank space where a bullet had shattered the glass.

Now, as the sun lifted, its light struck sparks off
tiny fragments on his jeans. He flicked them away
carefully. Before tumbling out of the shack he had
made sure to remove his wristwatch and anything
else that might catch light and betray him.

He knew who had fired the bullet. Inside the
shack, its cracked black cover freshly nicked by that
same projectile, lay a Bible as thick as a man's thigh,
its cream flyleaves scribbled over in old brown ink
with names of his forebears and the dates of their
lives and deaths going back to 1789, when an inden-
tured servant from Cornwall bought the book second-
hand in London and recorded the birth of a son
named Jotham. Four generations of names followed
before the simple entry: "Eben Candler, murdered
by Ezekiel Finlayson, Hawkins County, Kentucky,
May 11, 1882. His will be done." Eighteen similar
notations appeared on succeeding pages, in differing
hands, until the survivors wearied of keeping count.
The final line, "Jotham Edward Candler, born
September 8, 1951," written in his father's formal
script, commemorated his own birth. Finlayson losses
were not included.

No one remembered the specifics of that first
encounter between a Candler and a Finlayson,
although it had something to do with the ownership
of forty acres of bottom land in Unico County. Only
the casualties were remembered. Jotham's own

coming of age had been marked by a daily catechism in which he was expected to recite, in what ever order asked, the names of the Candler slain, their murderers, and the dates of their deaths as they had been recorded in the big Bible; and when he was strong enough to lift a squirrel rifle, he had been taught to think of his small, furry targets not as squirrels, but as Finlaysons.

It did not matter that no one knew who held title to those forty acres—that was as gone as the bottomland itself, seized by the bank during the depression of 1893—or that the fecundity of the Candler and Finlayson women had led to considerable interbreeding between the two families during the long truces. Hatred was an inheritance as solid and treasured as the old Bible and Great-Grandmother Candler's homely samplers, their red embroidery and white linen gone the same dead-skin brown on the walls of the tiny shack. Jotham, with a bachelor's degree in agriculture and three years in Vietnam behind him, was growing marijuana on plots that had supported his father's stills, and the Finlaysons had sold Ezekiel's ferrier's shop to buy a funeral home and the first of a chain of hardware stores, but aside from that little had changed. Bad blood was bad always.

As the sun cleared the mountain, its light turned leafy green coming down through the branches. Creatures stirred in the dry-shuck mattress of last year's leaves, and the last wisp of woodsmoke left the shack's chimney in a bit of shredded tissue that vanished into the thatch of fog now treetop-high as it lifted and broke apart. Jotham's assailant would know by that that he was no longer inside. The waiting was almost ended.

Jotham was the last Candler to bear that surname. His sisters were married and his only brother had died in Korea before Jotham was old enough to remember him. He would carry the name to the grave with him because of what the army's defoliants had done to his genes in Da Nang. In view of that temptation—the opportunity to wipe out by one death the long line of Candlers—young Bertram Finlayson's attempt to kill him in his sleep that morning seemed long overdue.

For he had no doubt it was Bertram. Eight years Jotham's junior, he had been too young to serve in Vietnam, and had spent that frustration in turkey shoots across the state, winning a caseful of trophies to display under the antlered heads on the walls of his fine house in town. His arsenal was a legend among collectors of firearms and he often boasted that he had used them to kill every kind of animal that lived in the county but one. He was the only Finlayson young enough and mean enough to bother about a fight that most had thought was buried with Jotham's father.

Several times since Jotham had returned from college, Bertram had tried to draw him into something in town, from which Jotham had always walked away. Witnesses said it was because he had had enough of killing in Asia. But those who said that were thinking of other wars, did not understand that the object of his had been to stay alive; killing came secondary, if at all. And now here he was, twelve years and ten thousand miles later, trying to stay alive in another jungle.

A squirrel began chattering, a high-pitched coughing noise like a small engine trying to start. Something was annoying it. Not him; the squirrel was too far away, high in an ash on the other side of the shack. He spotted its humped profile on the side of the trunk sixty feet up and scanned the ground at the base. A treefall twenty yards down the slope looked promising. He raised the 30.06 and lined up the iron sights and sent a bullet into the center of the fall. Something jumped, startled. Dead leaves rattled on the inert branches.

The echo of his first report was still snarling in the distance when he fired again, into those moving leaves. Almost instantly, a section of bark on a cedar a foot to Jotham's right exploded in a cloud of splinters, followed quickly by the crack of a .30-30. He hurled himself and his weapon headlong down the slope, rolling and coming up on the other side of a clump of suckers grown up around a pine stump. The squirrel had stopped chattering.

Bertram was a cooler hand than he'd thought. After the first shot he had waited, then fired at Jotham's second muzzle flash.

Again the waiting began.

Once, after exchanging fire with a Cong he had never seen, Jotham had waited for eleven hours in a fog of mosquitoes and heavy air, unmoving, his survival dependent upon his either killing the guerrilla or boring him into moving on. At the end the Cong had lost patience first, and when he rose from cover to investigate, Jotham had taken his head off with a burst from his M-16. How to wait was the hardest lesson of all. He settled himself on his other knee to give that haunch a rest.

The sun climbed into a thin sheeting of clouds that parted from time to time, changing the light as in an ancient motion picture. The air warmed, grew hot and thick. Twice he was attacked by wood ticks, once on the back of a hand, the other time, very painfully, on his neck. He did not move to brush them away. When the sun was directly overhead, he knew a terrible urge to get up and find out if Bertram was still there. More than the heat it made the sweat stand out in burrs on his forehead and greased his armpits and crotch. It must have been what the Cong felt just before he committed suicide.

But Jotham held his position and it subsided.

No one came up the mountain. In other years, uninvited visitors had met moonshiners' buckshot, and now even the authorities counseled against wandering the hills and chancing the protective wrath of marijuana growers and mad survivalists.

Around midafternoon the sky darkened and big

drops pattered the leaves on the ground and rolled along the edge of the bill of Jotham's cap and hung quivering before falling to his raised thigh with loud plops. He swung the rifle horizontal to keep moisture out of the barrel. But the rain passed swiftly. A rainbow arched over the shack and melted away.

The air cooled toward dusk. Bertram would have to move soon. Jotham's new knowledge of his enemy's instincts told him that he would not again risk darkness in the woods with an experienced jungle fighter. Jotham reversed legs again, working the stiffness out of the long muscles in his thighs.

The woods to the west were catching fire in the lowering sun when a buck muledeer that Jotham had never heard went crashing off through the woods on the opposite side of the shack, blatting a warning to others of its kind. At that moment the treefall shook and a pair of bull shoulders with a hatless head nestled in between reared against a sky striped with tree trunks. Light sheared along something long and shiny.

Jotham raised his rifle without aiming, trusting to the barrel to find its mark because he could no longer see the front sight, and touched the trigger. The butt pulsed against his shoulder, but he did not hear the blast. It had been that way when he'd killed the Cong. In roaring silence the bull shoulders hunched and the hatless head went back and the silhouette crumpled in on itself like a balloon deflating. The long and shiny thing flashed, falling.

Jotham let the sun slip to a red crescent before rising. In gray light he approached the treefall, lifting his feet clear of the old stumps more from memory than from sight, his eyes fixed on the dark thing draped over the treefall with the .30-30 on the ground in front of it. Carefully he used a foot to slide the rifle further out of the reach of the dangling hands, then took another step and grasped a handful of straw-colored hair and raised a slack face with open eyes and mouth into the last ray of light. It was Bertram Finlayson.

He let the face drop and started down the mountain toward town to tell his sister Lucy that she was a widow.

KATE

She was born Maria Katharina Horony on November 7, 1850, in Budapest, the first child of Katharina Boldizar of Debrecen and Michael Horony; and came to the United States with her parents and four surviving brothers and sisters in 1863, arriving in Davenport, Iowa, two days before her thirteenth birthday. A brother, Imre, had died of a fever at age four, and another, Julius, grew thin and pale in the tween-decks during the ocean crossing and finally faded into a dry husk that was sewn into sailcloth and weighted down with two hand-wrought fireplace dogs that had been in her father's family for a century and slid between the waves. Michael himself, the patriarch, bought a small farm and burst his heart between the potato rows seventeen months after their arrival. In the Horony family, Death was a hideous old uncle who came Sundays to drink the strong tea in the parlor and laid his bony hand on the knees of young and old and then left with apologies for his short stay and promises to return.

Mary Katharine, as she was then known, for the entire family had by that time passed through the crucible of Americanization, matured quickly, and at fourteen was often mistaken for a grown woman when she appeared in town with her mother on errands in mourning black. In the 1860s mourning was fashionable, and thanks to the Widow of White-hall and the alarming chain of coffins steaming up the rails from Manassas and Sharpsburg and Antietam and the Wilderness, the shop windows and cata-logues were strung with silks and broadcloth and velvet-palmed gloves becomingly cut and dyed with India ink; the stately adolescent, unaware then of the effect, cut an arresting figure on the streets of Daven-port in lace-trimmed black bonnet and cape and ankle shoes with onyx buttons ordered from Mont-gomery Ward. Her face in those years of comparative slimness was an exotic oval, not at all the moon it would become, her forehead high and domed, her eyes like an angelic little boy's, and her lips full and bent permanently into a smile in imitation of her mother, who believed that a pleasant expression prevented a face from aging. If she had the long thick nose of her Magyar forebears, that defect only added to the overall handsome mannishness of her appearance.

With young womanhood came stays, which squeezed an early tendency toward matronliness into the hourglass beloved of a healthy young nation with an overfondness for Rubens' cherubic nudes. A fascination with prints and colors asserted itself as soon as Michael Horony's memory was respectfully put down in camphor and cedar.

This coaxed a bloom not only from her cheeks but from her mother's as well, for the little income strained out of mulish earth by a widowed mother, a half-grown son, a distracted daughter, and three small children was not to be squandered on bright scarves and calico that cost as much as three bolt-ends of stout gingham. Her father's razor strap was employed almost as frequently during these years as it had been when he lived.

By then Mary Katherine had divined the meaning, if not precisely the import, of the looks she drew from men. Davenport was a major stop for steamers plying the Mississippi River, and although while in town her mother made certain that neither of them passed near the levee, Mary Katherine flushed at the appreciative expression that came in the otherwise poker faces of silk-hatted gamblers and the rubber, professionally cheerful faces of derbied drummers when she passed them farther inland and felt her mother's gloved hand tighten around hers and hasten her on past. She detected pomade and whiskey on their persons, smells associated with her father; and her veins ran warm.

One month before her seventeenth birthday Mary Katherine dressed for town; and if Katharina

Horony thought her daughter's cape too much for the balmy early-autumn climate, she made no mention of it. If she had, Mary Katherine had a cough handy by way of explanation, although not severe enough to banish her indoors, as that would have made it all for nothing. For under the cape she wore her best dress over another one more serviceable, two petticoats, and three pairs of drawers, enough clothing to fill the small portmanteau she had elected to leave behind for want of a way to smuggle it into town.

Her chance came in the mercantile when her mother was comparing cloves of garlic under the patient eye of the proprietor behind the counter. Wandering toward a stack of ladies' hats in the corner next to the dress material, Mary Katherine pretended interest in the dyed ostrich plumes, then when the merchant turned away to weigh the cloves, opened the door carefully so as not to disturb the bell looped to the handle and left the store. From there she ran the three blocks to the levee as fast as two legs bound in five layers of linen would let her. There the *US Oleander* was loading. For an anxious hall- hour while she knew her mother was looking for her she stood among the passengers waiting to board, then eased onto the bottom deck while the man taking tickets was arguing with a fat woman who insisted that her son, nearly six feet tall with a blue shadow on his chin, was under twelve and so eligible to ride hall-fare.

The bottom deck was an adventure in odors. For

a girl reared near a port, there was nothing novel about the smells of baled jute and molasses in barrels and freshly sawn lumber; but when they came together with various fine scents emanating from parasoled women on the arms of men in striped vests and planters' hats, with water slapping the hollow hull and the boat actually shifting beneath her own tread when she crossed the deck, they assumed an enchantment befitting the oils of China. The aroma was not to be matched and had only to be encountered again to return an aging fancy- woman to a youth in which nothing was beyond reach

She was, however, dismayed to learn that even on this fine whitewashed craft with its great painted paddles floating gently astern, the stench of fish overlay everything, from the barrels of salted salmon resting in the hold. It reminded her unpleasantly of the voyage across the ocean and of her brother Julius quietly dying in his rope hammock.

But the past was no fit opponent for the present. The throated steam whistle, often heard in town but never before from directly overhead, with its vibration buzzing beneath the soles of her feet, opened the future.

A deckhand closed it. After observing her for some minutes wandering unescorted between the decks, he asked to see her ticket, and when she took too long searching for it in her tiny reticule he escorted her to the bridge. The pilot was a red-bearded man in his forties with a long brown face under a beetle-black derby, a joint of charred bulldog pipe nailed into the center of his face, and a tan leather coat with distressed elbows worn over a pinstripe shirt without a collar.

He, too, had a fishy smell, like everything else aboard except the passengers.

Standing at the wheel he heard the deckhand's report, interrupting him once to reach up and tug the whistle, then dismissed him.

"What's your name, lass?"

He had a thick, burring speech from which she had to sort the words before she answered.

"Kate."

"What's your surname, Kate, lass?"

The glassed-in cabin was strong with him. "Fish."

"Fish?"

"Fisher. I'm Kate Fisher."

He rotated the wheel slightly. His pipe gurgled. "Well, Kate Fisher, lass, what are we to do with ye?"

"I'll work for my passage."

"I have all the hands I require."

"You won't take me back." It wasn't a question.

"I would were that my inclination, but I've a ruddy schedule to make." His softening of the "sch" put her in mind of the English sailors among the crew during the Atlantic crossing. But he wasn't English. "I would put ye ashore in Saint Looey did I not ken ye'd be raped and your white throat slit five minutes after we put off. The war took its toll of gentlemen, ye see."

"I am twenty-one and can care for myself."

"Ye're eighteen or younger, or I'm no judge." He gave the whistle two short blasts and corrected course around a float full of fishermen. "Are ye Catholic, Kate Fisher?"

She wondered if Roman Catholics had a smell of their own, and if it was as evident to him as his was to her. "Yes."

"I've a place for ye, then. Now get below and tell that ruddy barbarian Isherwood he's to keep his sweaty paws off ye until we land. In a nice way, mind. He killed a woman in Hannibal and he has terrible bad nightmares aboot it."

She never found out if he was joshing about the deckhand. When the boat docked in St. Louis the pilot took her inland to a great stone building behind an evil-looking cathedral as large as downtown Davenport and then he passed out of her life forever.

She never learned his name, but in later years, when whiskey and memory overtook her, she would smirk at his bluff innocence and despise him.

The mother superior of the convent was a fat Frenchwoman of indeterminate age with a nose twice the size of hers with an angry red boil on the side of it and a mustache. She gave Kate—for from then on Mary Katherine was never known by any other name—to a very tall, very thin woman in a nun's habit, who took her to another room where she was made to strip and climb into a wooden tub full of cold water and grasp her ankles while Sister scrubbed her back with brown soap and a coarse cloth until it stung. A bucket of icy water was dumped over her head and she toweled off shivering with thin terry and put on clean drawers—not her comfortable linen ones but a pair made of gray shoddy that chafed her thighs—and a plain white cotton shift.

Sitting on a wormwood bench she pulled on coarse black knee-length stockings secured with plain garters and laced on a pair of man's scuffed brown brogans that extended two inches past her toes and felt corrugated inside.

When Sister advanced on her with steel shears she tried to run, but the thin woman was faster and much stronger and sat her on the bench with an arm wrench that made her cry out. She was still recovering from it when her wet black hair was gathered in a wiry fist and cut off at the nape of her neck with three crunching snips. No mirrors were allowed in the convent, and when that night she was locked in a ward with a dozen other shorn girls who spoke among themselves in whispers and stared at her without addressing her, she lay on her narrow cot crying, convinced she looked a horror. A few days later, however, when she was allowed to pass under Sister's escort through the courtyard into the cathedral, she admired the boyishly ethereal face framed in a scarf looking back at her from the surface of the holy water. Although she genuflected and hurried to a pew before Sister could box her ears for the sin of

Vanity, on her knees she determined never to let her hair grow back out.

Big Nose Kate was born in the convent. The other girls called her that from the time they learned her name, and tailored jokes to her that were previously reserved for Mother Superior's fearsome fistulated snout. The first time a girl used the name to her face, Kate knocked her down and straddled her and clawed at her eyes until Sister separated and whipped them both across their bare buttocks until they bled.

Nevertheless it quickly became popular, and even the nuns came to use it to distinguish her from the other two Kates in their charge.

So Big Nose Kate came out of that time, but more than just the name. On occasions later when the clergy got in the way of her vocation she would claim that the only difference between God's house and a whorehouse was the pointed roof, and those who heard would think she was merely trying to shock them, but what she never spoke of was the Private Instruction in Sister's cell. There among the hymnals and Latin dictionaries and votive candles she discovered that the reason nuns never squirmed like the girls under the scratching of their shoddy drawers was that they never wore them.

The diet in the convent was mostly salmon from the riverboats, and Sister tasted of it, so that despite the irony of her adopted surname Kate never ate fish the rest of her life.

After hours the girls practiced what they had learned from Sister with one another in their cots. Although Kate often took part, she gained far more knowledge than release from these sessions. For her the convent would be a lesson in the universal craving for physical fulfillment that she would carry to the grave.

There were only two ways to get out of the convent.

Escape was not one. The first week Kate was there, a sixteen-year-old girl whose baby had been remanded to an orphanage downriver slipped out of the cathedral while Sister was in holy rapture and was gone two days and one night. She attempted to sneak aboard a riverboat, was found out, and scrambled down the levee a hop ahead of the out-of-shape deckhand who pursued her and lost his footing and her trail at the bottom. On the second day a city policeman caught her picking through a trash barrel behind a restaurant, recognized the dirty convent shift she was wearing, and delivered her to Sister, who attended her lovingly during her long recovery from Sister's whipping. Other attempts were made while Kate was in residence, but none came even that close to success, although the punishment was the same. The St. Louis city fathers were staunchly Catholic and the police were always willing to aid in recapturing runaways.

Coming of age was the first of the sanctioned roads to freedom. Upon reaching twenty-one, the petitioner had the choice of entering the novitiate or leaving by the front door. A surprising number opted for the former, and Kate could always identify these among the novices who spelled the nuns in the classroom and kept order in the dormitory, by their broken wills. She herself had no intention of letting that happen to her, or of spending the next four years begging carbolic off the nuns for her abraded thighs and tasting salmon in Sister's cell. The second key to liberty—of a sort—was marriage.

One of the convent's unadvertised purposes was to serve as a kind of animal shelter for pioneers looking for wives. Several times a week, men stuffed into high boots and new suits of clothes tramped through the classroom and dormitory to look at the girls and talk with some of them. Mother Superior said they were settlers inspecting the spiritual arrangements before putting down stakes in the area, but no one was taken in by it and Mother Superior herself made no great effort to be convincing. Kate talked with a few of the men, but was offended by the blunt way they studied her build under her shift and by the sour earthen smell of them, and they in turn lost interest when their questions about her people went unanswered. Their wills, moreover, were as strong as hers if not stronger, something she had had quite enough of from her mother and from Sister. If they were shopping, she was too. When Sister noted her attitude and rebuked her during Private Instruction for the sin of Pride, Kate feigned ignorance, and rather than allow herself to be backed into admitting the true purpose of the visitations, the thin woman merely clenched her long jaw and raised her habit.

Once a month the girls' teeth were inspected by a dentist named Silas Melvin.

Melvin was a fussy little man with a pink face and rimless spectacles and black hair receding into a half-moon four inches above his eyebrows, although he was still in his twenties. He affected a laughable fastidiousness of dress in view of his shabby coat and turned collars that convinced the other girls, who called him Aunt Silas, that their sex held no interest for him. Kate was less sure and settled the point one day by borrowing a shift from a girl several sizes smaller and arching her back so that her nipples stood out against the taut cotton while he was leaning over to look inside her mouth, causing him to drop his little mirror and crack the glass.

She liked his clean smell. He admired her "Greek profile" and said she had fine teeth. Mostly she liked the fact that he was plainly afraid of Sister and avoided her as much as he could without offending. A man who could be intimidated represented freedom.

Kate encouraged his attentions, and soon he was making his visits twice a month, blaming an outbreak of pyorrhea in the city. No one credited it. By then it was commonly accepted that Aunt Silas was smitten with Big Nose Kate.

Mother Superior blessed the match. Professional

men were a sturdy influence on rebellious young women. Moreover, despite the fact that his stubborn Protestantism precluded their marrying inside the Church, Mother Superior was serene in its teachings and believed it would encompass them both in time; which made it a victory of Faith.

So it was that six months after Kate came to the convent, she was wed by the pastor of the Presbyterian church.

Dr. and Mrs. Silas Melvin booked steamboat passage on the Mississippi, she no longer a stowaway but a large handsome woman in stays and taffeta with a flat flowered hat pinned to her short hair, part of a modest trousseau presented to her by an admiring husband. At Vicksburg, a town rising slowly from mortar-smashed rubble and blasted trees, they transferred to a sleeper car and clattered over polished steel through scorched fields tangled with the rusty twisted corpses of old rails torn up by Sherman's troops on the way to Atlanta. There the couple settled.

In the late 1860s that town was still reeling from Sherman. Most of the burned blocks had been cleared, but for the rest of Kate's life the stench of char would remind her of her first marriage. Widows took in washing, and so many backyards were crisscrossed with burdened clotheslines she wondered that any men were left in Atlanta. But they were in the streets, straggle-haired and bitten-bearded in rags of Confederate shoddy with sockets for eyes and stumps on display and filthy palms outstretched. At night they grew fangs and preyed on their daytime benefactors in alleys stinking of slops. For all that, Atlanta was rebuilding. Professional men were desperately needed, but because no one could afford to pay for their services they were rare. Soon after Silas nailed up his shingle he had a full practice. Although there was no money, the Melvins dined on pork pies and fresh fish and venison roasts and baskets of eggs and flasks of milk brought by his patients. Kate gained weight rapidly.

Before long it became evident that the rich food was not to be blamed for this.

Concerned when his wife became too ill mornings to eat breakfast, Silas brought home a doctor who had served as surgeon with General Bragg and who examined her and congratulated them both while accepting a large apple pie in lieu of his fee.

She bore him a son.

The son died.

No one knew why he died. Not Kate, who bathed and cared for him as lovingly as she tended Silas's instruments, which had to be boiled on the cookstove in the kitchen between usings, and the basin that had to be scoured of blood and iodine. Not Melvin, who wanted to send the boy to Baltimore to learn dentistry as soon as he was through with public school and looked to the day when he would be Old Doc Melvin to his son's Young Doc Melvin. Certainly not the doctor, who signed the death certificate and shook his head and said that the war was still claiming victims in Atlanta. Baptized Presbyterian, the boy could not be buried out of the Catholic Church as Kate requested, but the local priest, a patient of Silas's, agreed to preside at a secular ceremony in the couple's house, after which a Presbyterian minister officiated at graveside.

Silas died soon after. Yellow fever was sweeping the city, and as the symptoms were in keeping with the disease, Bragg's old surgeon wrote it on the certificate. Kate knew it wasn't that, or even the broken heart suggested by the doctor in private. It was Uncle Death come back to pay his respects to her family.

Industry had come to Atlanta, and with it northern money. Kate buried Silas next to their son and sold their house and his practice to a dentist from Vermont with a birdlike wife and three pale children and went west. As she watched the green southern scenery sliding past the train window she could not know that she was tracing the steps of another Atlanta exile whom Uncle Death had compelled to leave some months earlier, a dentist like Silas, although that was where the resemblance ended, as indeed it did to anyone else she would ever know.

When they met, the year was 1877 and the place was a clabber of adobe dugouts and unpainted shacks swept up against the base of Government Hill below Fort Griffin, Texas. He was a picket-thin man of twenty-five, with a phlegmy cough and a preference for colored shirts and gray suits of good material that flapped on him. She was Big Nose Kate, hefty at twenty-seven and developing a roll under her chin but a long way from fat, and working John Shanssey's saloon on a financial arrangement with the beetle-browed ex-pugilist. Dentists were an interest, and although this one had swung a board from the peak of his tent on the edge of town with JOHN HENRY HOLLIDAY, D.D.S., inexpertly painted on it, he spent most of his time playing poker and dealing faro in Shanssey's. The men with whom he played were all big and filthy and stank of guts, but they bought their chips with fist-size wads of crisp bills obtained from the Fort Griffin paymaster in return for buffalo hides. The kill was so lush that year they lost hundreds of dollars and got up from the table lurching and laughing. Sometimes they didn't but the way Holliday played, smiling as he pulled in the chips and telling nigger jokes in his soft drawl and sipping frequently from the tumbler of whiskey that was always at his elbow, the mood around the table remained guardedly genial.

She began as his partner. Some of the buffalo runners had wives and sweethearts back in civilization for whom they held back hide money not required for food and supplies. It was her role to make their acquaintance and get them to buy her drinks and jolly them into trying to double and treble those reserves. Kate was good with the quiet ones. She charmed and bullied and shamed and groped at them—for she had learned a long time before that a man who was drunk and aroused was more likely to spend money than one who was just drunk—and Sister's Private Instruction had taught her that no oath was equal to the demands of the body. And if, after dropping the earnings of an entire season's shooting and skinning on the turn of a pasteboard, a player showed signs of becoming truculent, a trip upstairs with Kate was usually all that was required to put him back on his feet, as Doc put it. For this she received a cut of the winnings after Shanssey had sliced his off the top.

At sunup they went back to Doc's tent, where she rubbed his back with alcohol and held his head when his coughing gutted him and lay with him when he had the strength for it. He was a fitful lover, stronger than he looked, and he kept at it with the same concentration he displayed at his table until he exploded and then collapsed wheezing.

When he stirred she would have a tumbler ready for him and he would drink it off in two swallows and go to sleep. Her business fell off after that. She knew it was because the other Fort Griffin men, who spent all day with their bare arms inside buffalo carcasses to the shoulders and made breastworks of them when the Comanches came looking to strip off their skins, were afraid of catching what Doc had from her. She didn't care. Doc's action supported them both, and caring for him when he was low fed something in her that had been cheated when her son and husband died so suddenly.

Every afternoon that Doc climbed out of his roll to put on a fresh shirt and take his place behind the cue box in Shanssey's was ground held against the terrible uncle. They shared secrets insofar as their self-protective natures allowed. Once when drinking he told her of his cousin in an Atlanta convent—she recognized the name of her alma mater's old rival—to whom he still wrote letters, and beat Kate up for mentioning it when he was sober. After that she didn't bring it up again, even at times when he looked at her and she knew she was being measured against the angel of the Lord back home and felt the urge to enlighten him as to what went on in convents. It wasn't fear. If she gave any thought to such things at all, she would suppose that she loved Doc.

Kate wasn't present in the saloon when Doc and Ed Bailey fell out. Bailey was a buffalo runner and a sometime scout for the army who wore an issue Colt's in a cavalry scabbard with the strap unbuttoned. Doc caught him looking at the deadwood—sneaking a peek at Doc's discards during poker—and admonished him quietly to "play poker," which was the gentleman's way of asking an opponent to refrain from cheating. Bailey withdrew his hand from the pile, drew two cards from the deck, then resumed his inspection of Doc's deadwood. When Doc laid the cards face down and began pulling in the pot, Bailey challenged him, his hand dropping under the table. Doc jerked a pearl-handled knife from his inside breast pocket and eviscerated him.

A marshal's deputy was present, and threw down on Doc and relieved him of the knife and two pistols while Bailey was still trying to keep his entrails from spilling over his belt. Doc was removed to a hotel while a wagon was readied to take him to the Shackleford County seat at Albany for a hearing.

The story that got told later was full of lynch mobs and vigilantes and had Kate dressing up in man's clothes and setting fire to a stable and then taking Doc away at gunpoint from the deputy left to guard him while the others were fighting the fire. The part about the man's clothes and the fire was true enough, but they were just gestures to keep the glare off the deputy, an old customer whom Kate paid a hundred dollars to watch the blaze outside the window while she and Doc walked out. At dawn John Shanssey brought two horses to the cottonwoods by Collins Creek where the fugitives were hiding. From there they rode four hundred miles to Dodge City, Kansas, where cowboys were squalling for more games to lose money on and where Doc had a friend named Earp.

That was four years ago. Kate missed Dodge; not the town itself, clapboard huts on a grass street studded with cow flop, and certainly not the profitable understanding Doc had as a gambler with Wyatt Earp, a man she distrusted, on the local police force, but rather the several weeks during which Doc practiced dentistry for real out

of a walk-up office and introduced Kate to

acquaintances as Mrs. Holliday. It all blew up when
Doc stopped coming home nights, staying up
drinking with Wyatt's kid brother Morgan and
betting on whether the next man through the door of
the Long Branch would be wearing a kerchief or a
cravat. She and Doc fought over it. He broke her
nose; she clawed his face and decamped for Ogallala.
He said she'd be back. She said he'd write begging her
to come back. They were both right. He would get in
a bad way and write her in his fine hand—always
immaculate, whether he was drunk or sober—saying
he needed her, and she would respond by returning.
It was a pattern they would repeat in Colorado, New
Mexico, and Arizona, with Uncle following them all
the way. He and Doc were old acquaintances.

The first time she left him in Tombstone, Kate
had gone to the copper-mining center of Glove and
spent the five hundred dollars he had given her on a
down payment on a hotel, which became a whorehouse with very little alteration and an arrangement
with the girls that pleased everyone. During her
reunion with Doc she had left the books in care of her
brightest girl. Despite detailed instructions the girl
had made a mess of them, wandering outside Kate's
carefully ruled lines and getting the debits mixed up
with the credits or just plain neglecting to record
transactions, and since her return Kate had been
involved in reconstructing the past month's finances.
That the girl had been robbing her blind was a
certainty, but she couldn't concentrate long enough

to determine by how much. Her eye was still tender where Doc had hit her this time and her bruised ribs hurt when she moved or drew a deep breath. Worse, she felt guilty for having left him with the investigation into the deaths on Fremont Street still pending.

That was why, when the mail came bearing a letter in the familiar flowing hand, she got up so quickly to accept it the pain doubled her.

November 5, 1881

Dear Kate,

Well, they have got me in jail again...

HELL ON THE DRAW

I n the weeks to come there would be considerable debate and some brandishing of weapons over who had been the first to lay eyes on Mr. Nicholas Pitt of Providence; but the fact of the matter is the honor belonged to Ekron Fast, Persephone's only blacksmith. It was he, after all, who replaced the shoe the stranger's great black hammerhead had thrown just outside town, and as everyone who lived there knew, a traveler's first thought upon reaching water or civilization in that dry Huachuca country was his horse. Nor was Pitt's a horse for a former cow man like Ekron to forget.

"Red eyes," he declared to the gang at the Fallen Shaft that Wednesday night in July. "Eighteen—hell, twenty hands if he was one, that stud, with nary a speck of any color but black on him except for them eyes. Like burning pipe-plugs they was. Feature that."

"Oklahoma Blood Eye." Gordy Wolf, bartender at the Shaft, refilled Ekron's glass from a measured bottle, collected his coin, and made a note of the transaction in the ledger with a gnawed stub of pencil. As a half-breed Crow he couldn't drink, and so the owner required him to keep track of what came out of stock. "I seen it in McAlester. Thisyer dun mare just up and rolled over on the cavalry sergeant that was riding her, snapped his neck like dry rot. Your Mr. Pip better watch that don't happen to him."

"Fermented mash, more'n likely, both cases." This last came courtesy of Dick Wagner, who for the past eleven years had stopped off at the Shalt precisely at 6:45 for one beer on his way home from the emporium. He chewed sensen in prodigious amounts to keep his wife Lucy from detecting it on his breath.

"Pitt, not Pip," said Ekron. "Mr. Nicholas Pitt of Providence. Where's that?"

"East a ways," Wagner said. "Kansas I think."

"He didn't talk like no Jayhawker I ever heard. 'There's a good fellow,' he says to me, and gives me that there ten-cent piece."

"This ain't no ten-cent piece." Gordy Wolf was staring at the coin Ekron had given him for the drink. It had a wavy edge and had been stamped crooked with the likeness of nobody he recognized. He bit it.

"Might I see it?"

Gordy Wolf now focused his good eye on Professor the Doctor Webster Bennett, late of the

New York University classical studies department, more lately of the Brimstone Saloon across the street. The bartender's hesitation did not mean he suspected that the coin would not be returned; he was just unaccustomed to having the good educator conscious at that hour. Professor the Doctor Bennett's white linen and carefully brushed broadcloth had long since failed to conceal from anyone in Persephone that beneath it, at any hour past noon, was a sizable bag.

Handed the piece, Professor the Doctor Bennett stroked the edge with this thumb, then raised his chin from the bar and studied the coin on both sides, at one point holding it so close to his pinkish right eye he seemed about to screw it in like a monocle. Finally he returned it.

"Roman. Issued, I would say, sometime after the birth of Christ, and not very long after. The profile belongs to Tiberius."

"It cover Ekron's drink?"

"I rather think it will." He looked at Ekron. "I would hear more of your Mr. Pitt."

"He ain't *my* Mr. Pitt. Anyway I don't much look at folks, just the animals they ride in on. Seen his clothes; fine city ones they was, and a duster. Hogleg tied down on his hip like you read in the nickel novels. And there's something else."

"Gunfighter?" Wagner sat up straight. His greatest regret, aside from having chosen Lucy for his helpmeet, was that he had come West from Louisiana too late to see a real gunfight. The great pistoleers were all dead or gone East to act on the stage. All except one, of course, and he had proved frustrating.

"Or a dude," said Gordy Wolf. "Tenderfoot comes out here, wants everyone to think he's Wild Bill."

Ekron spat, missing the cuspidor by his standard margin. "Forget the damn gun, it don't count. Leastwise not till it goes off. Gordy, you're injun. Man comes in off that desert country up north. Babocomari's dry till September, Tucson's a week's ride, gila and roadrunner's the only game twixt here and Iron Springs. What you figure he's got to have in provisions and truck?"

"Rifle, box of cartridges. Grain for the horse. Bacon for himself and maybe some canned goods. Two canteens or a skin. That's if he's white. Apache'd do with the rifle and water."

"Well, Mr. Nicholas Pitt of Providence didn't have none of that."

"What you mean, just water?"

"I mean nothing. Not water nor food nor rifle nor even a blanket to roll to keep the chill off his cojones in the desert at night. Man rides in with just his hip gun and saddle and nary a bead of sweat on man nor mount, and him with nothing behind him but a hunnert miles of sand and alkali." He jerked down his whiskey and looked around at his listeners. "Now, what would you call a man like that, if not the Devil his own self?"

Thus, in addition to having been first to spot the stranger who would mean so much to the town's fortunes, Ekron Fast settled upon him the appellation by which he would be commonly known when not directly addressed. From that time forward, His Own Self, uttered in silent but generally agreed-upon capitals, meant none other and required no illumination.

At the very moment that this unconscious christening was taking place, Guy Dante, manager at the Belial Hotel, was in the throes of a similar demonstration, albeit with somewhat less theater, for his wife. Angel Dante had come in perturbed to have found Dick Wagner gone and the emporium closed and therefore a trip wasted to purchase red ink with which to keep the books. As was his custom, Guy had been bleating on while she unpinned her hat and removed her gloves, and so went unheeded for the crucial first minute of his speech.

"...registered with no mark like I ever saw, and him from his clothes and deportment a city gentleman who should certainly have enjoyed a considerable education," he finished.

"What mark? What gentleman? Oh, Mr. Dante, sometimes I believe you talk sideways just to increase my burden." She tugged on green velvet pen-wipers for another go at the books.

"Room six. He registered while you were out. I just sent Milton up with water for his bath. Weren't you listening?"

She didn't acknowledge the question. In truth she

was slightly hard of hearing and preferred to have people think she was rude rather than advertise the fact that she was seven years older than her husband; a piece of enlightenment that would have surprised many of the town's citizens, who assumed that the difference was much greater. "I don't smell the stove," she said.

"He said cold water would be more than satisfactory. Here's his mark I was telling you about." He shoved the registration book at her.

She seated her spectacles in the dents alongside her nose and examined the two- pronged device scratched deeply into the creamy paper. She ran a finger over it. "It looks like some kind of brand. He must be a cattleman."

"He didn't look like one. What would a cattleman be doing in this country?"

"Perhaps he knows something. Perhaps the railroad is coming and he's here to check out the prospects for shipping beef. Oh, Mr. Dante, why did you give him six? Nine's the presidential."

"He asked for six."

"Land. I hope you had the presence to have Milton carry up his traps."

"He didn't have any. And he didn't talk like any cattleman either. He asked about the Brimstone. Wanted to know if it's for sale."

"An entrepreneur, in Persephone?" She cast a glance up the stairs, removing her spectacles as if the portly, diamond-stickpinned figure she associated with an entrepreneur might appear on the landing and see them. "Land. He must know something."

"If he does, this town sure isn't it. Nor Ned Harpy. He'd sell his sister before he'd let that saloon go. And for a smaller price to boot."

"Nevertheless we must make him comfortable. Prosperity may be involved."

Dante made that braying noise his wife found distressing. "I hope he tells us when it's fixed to start. Wait till you see what he gave me for the room."

Only the manager's familiar bray rose above the first floor, where Milton heard it on his way to room six. Inside he hung up the fine striped suit he had finished brushing and asked the man splashing behind the screen if he wanted his boots blacked as well.

Milton made beds, served meals, and banished dirt and dust from the Belial with an industry that came naturally to the son of a stablehand.

"If you would, lad." The man's whispery voice barely rose above the lapping in the tub. It reminded Milton of a big old rattler shucking its skin. "There's something on the bureau for you. Much obliged." Then he laughed, which was worse than when he spoke.

Milton picked up the boots, handsome black ones with butter-soft tops that flopped over and a curious two-pointed design on each one that looked like a cow's hoofprint. They were made of a wonderful kind of leather he had never seen or felt before, as dark as his father's skin. His skin was much lighter than his father's. He knew that some mean folks around town said he wasn't Virgil's son at all, sired as like as not by some unparticular plantation owner— disregarding that Milton was only thirteen and born well after Mr. Lincoln did his duty. Such folks could go to hell.

He got a chill then, in that close room in July in Arizona, and took his mind off it by examining the strange coin he had picked up from the dresser. Confederate pewter, most like. No wonder Mr. Pitt had laughed.

Only he didn't think that was the reason.

Damn little about strangers made sense—those few that found their way here after the last of the big silver interests had hauled its wagon east—but this one less than most.

Where were his possibles? Why weren't his clothes caked and stinking of man and horse, instead of just dusty? And how was it, after Milton had filled the bathtub himself with buckets of water ice-cold from the pump, that steam was rolling out under the screen where the stranger was bathing?

Josh Marlowe rode up from Mexico in the middle of a September rainstorm with water funneling off his hatbrim fore and aft and shining on his black oilskin. Charon's hoofs splashed mud up over his boots and made sucking sounds when they pulled clear. The gray snorted its misery.

Josh concurred. In times past he had preferred

entering a town in weather that kept folks indoors. There were some short fuses then who'd throw down on him the second they recognized him but wouldn't later when they had a chance to think of it, making arrivals the most dangerous time in a gunman's experience. But that was before he'd given up the road. Persephone was home, and now that there was no danger he discovered he hated riding in the rain.

Peaceable though he was these days, he clung to his old custom of coming in the back way. He dismounted behind the livery, found the back door locked, stepped back, and kicked it until Virgil opened it from inside. He stood there like always with coal-oil light at his back and his old Colt's Dragoon gleaming in his big black fist.

"Virgil, how many times I tell you to snuff that lantern when a stranger comes?"

The stablehand's barn-door grin shone in the bad light. He stuck the big pistol under his belt. "Balls, Mr. Josh. You ain't no stranger."

Josh left the point short of argument and handed him the reins. "How's Milton?"

"Gettin' uppity. Hotel work's got him thinking he's town folks." He led the gray
inside.

The barrel stove was glowing. Josh slung his saddle and pouches over an empty stall and warmed his hands. When he turned to put heat on his backside he spotted the black standing in its stall. He whistled. Reflection from the fire made its eyes look red.

"That there's Mr. Pitt's horse." Virgil began rubbing down Charon with burlap. "You stand clear of that animal, Mr. Josh. He's just plain evil."

"Who might Mr. Pitt be?"

"That's right, you been gone."

"Two months trailing grandee beef to Mexico City. This Pitt with the railroad? Credit won't acquire a mount like that."

"If he is, the railroad done bought the Brimstone. Mr. Pitt he runs the place now."

"Horseshit. Ned Harpy told me he'd die before he sold out."

"I reckon he wasn't pulling your leg." Josh saw the stablehand wasn't smiling. "The hell you say."

The black horse reared, screamed, plunged, and kicked its stall. The hammering mingled with a loud peal of thunder. Even Charon shied from it.

"You see what I mean about that animal," Virgil said when it had calmed down. "It happened real quick, Mr. Josh. Mr. Ned he got mad when that Mr. Pitt wouldn't take no as an answer and pulled on him right there in the gameroom. Only Mr. Pitt filled his hand first and just drilled that man full of holes. He was dead when he hit the floor. Mrs. Harpy she sold out and went back East."

"Ned was fast."

"Near as fast as you." Virgil was grave. "You stay

out of the Brimstone, Mr. Josh." He grinned. "Save that talk for your boy. I gave all that up years ago."

"I hope so, Mr. Josh. I surely does. You can't beat that man. Nobody can."

From there Josh went to the Fallen Shaft, where he closed the door against the wind and rain and piano music clattering out of the Brimstone. Gordy Wolf was alone. He took his elbows off the bar.

"Josh Marlowe. Gouge out my eyes and pour vinegar in the holes if it ain't. What can I draw you, Josh?"

"Tanglefoot. Where is everybody?" He slapped water off his hat and hooked a heel over the rail.

Gordy Wolf shook his head, poured, and made a mark in the ledger. "You could touch off a Hotchkiss in here since they put the piano in across the street. Nobody'd mind."

"What about the Professor the Doctor Webster Bennett? He'd never desert the Shaft."

"He's give up the Creature. Says it don't fit with teaching school."

"That's what the council said when they booted him for falling on his face during sums. They had closed down the schoolhouse."

"Mr. Pitt bought it and opened it back up. Professor the Doctor ain't got but six pupils and one of them's near as old as him. Way he struts and fluffs his feathers you'd think he's still learning Eyetalian and Greek to them rich men's sons back home."

"This the same Pitt killed Ned Harpy?"

"If there's two I'd hear about it."

"From what Virgil said I didn't take him to be one for the community."

"Before the school he bought the Belial Hotel from Old Man Merry and deeded it to Guy and Angel Dante and then he bought the emporium from Dick Wagner and made him manager at the Brimstone."

"I can't feature Lucy Wagner sitting still for that."

"Lucy went back to New Orleans. She got on worse with Mr. Pitt than she did with Dick. You wouldn't know Dick now. He's got him a red vest and spats."

"What's Pitt's purpose? When the mines played out I gave Persephone five years."

"He told Ekron Fast there's future here. Then he bought him a new forge with an autymobile."

"Ain't no autymobiles twixt here and Phoenix."

"There's one now. 'Thisyer's the future I been telling you about,' he says to Ekron. 'Master it.' Ekron run it straight into an arroyo. But he fixed it with his new *forge*."

"I reckon he's one stranger who's made himself popular," Josh said.

"He's got him an eye for what every man he meets wants more'n anything, plus a pocket deep enough to get it for him."

"Except Ned Harpy."

"Nobody much liked Ned anyway. If Mr. Pitt

was to run for mayor tomorrow I reckon he'd get everybody's vote but two."

"How is it he ain't throwed his loop over you and Virgil?"

The half-breed put an elbow on the bar and leaned in close enough for Josh to discover that his ledger-keeping had not prevented him from sampling the Shaft's stock. "On account of Virgil's a Christian man," he said. "And on account of I ain't. Mr. Pitt he gets what falls between."

"That's heathen talk."

"It ain't neither. Just because they throwed me out of the mission school after a week don't mean I didn't hear what they had to teach."

Josh drank whiskey. "I got to meet this fellow."

"How long's it been since you wore a pistol?" Gordy Wolf kept his good eye on him. "Three years."

"You'd best not."

"Talking's all I'm after."

"When your kind meet his kind it don't stop at talking."

"What kind's mine, Christian or Ain't?"

"I seen you struggling with both."

He stopped grinning and drained his glass. "It's a damn shame the mission school didn't keep you, Gordy. You'd of made a right smart preacher."

"Call me what you like. I'm just saying you'd best climb on that gray horse and ride out and forget all about Persephone. That Mr. Pitt is hell on the draw."

Thunder cracked.

Two months was hardly long enough for the Brimstone to change as much as it had since Josh's last visit. It was one thing to cover the knotty walls with scarlet cloth and take down the prizefighter prints behind the bar to make room for a gilt-framed painting of a reclining naked fat lady holding an apple and laughing; quite another to rip out the old pine bar and replace it with one made from gnarled black oak with what looked like horned evil children carved into the corners. Such items, like the enormous chandelier that now swung from the center rafter, its thousand candles filling the room with oppressive heat, required more time than that to order and deliver. Let alone make, for what catalog house stocked statuary representing serpents amorously entwined with more naked femininity like the two Amazons thus engaged on either side of the batwing doors?

Mr. Pitt's tastes were apparently not excessive for Persephone's nightlife, however.

The main room was packed. Under an awning of lazily turning smoke the drinkers' voices rose above the noise from the piano, where a thickish man in a striped suit and derby was playing something fit to raise blisters on a stump. The strange fast melody was unknown to Josh, who decided he had been below the border a mite too long.

"Look what the wind blew up from Mexico!"

Gordy Wolf hadn't lied about the spats and red vest. They were accompanied by green silk sleeve garters, a platinum watch chain and a dyed rabbit's-foot fob, and an eastern straw hat tipped forward at such a steep angle the former merchant had to slant his head back to see in front of him.

"Howdy, Dick." Josh sentenced his hand to serious pumping by one heavy with rings.

"What you think of the old place?" Dick Wagner asked. His eyes looked wild and he was grinning to his molars.

"Talks up for itself, don't it?"

"Loud and proud. Lucy'd hate it to death." He roared and clapped a hand on Josh's shoulder. "Keep! Draw one on the house from my gunslinging friend here."

"After I talk to the owner. He around?"

"That's him banging the pianny."

Josh stared at the derbied piano player. He was built like a nailkeg and very fair—a fact that surprised Josh, though he could not own why—and wore jaunty reddish chin-whiskers that put the former gunman in mind of an elf he had seen carved on the door of Irish Mike's hospitable house in St. Louis. As Josh approached him he turned glass-blue eyes on the newcomer. "I'll warrant you're Marlowe." He went on playing the bizarre tune.

"I reckon news don't grow much grass in a town this size."

"Nor does your reputation. I am Nicholas Pitt, originally of Providence. You'll excuse me for not clasping hands."

"It sounds a difficult piece."

"A little composition of my own. But it's not the reason. I only touch flesh with someone when we've reached accord."

Something in Pitt's harsh whisper made Josh grateful for this eccentricity. "I admired your horse earlier this evening."

"Beelzebub? I've had him forever. Ah, thank you, Margaret. Can I interest you in a libation, Marlowe?" He quit playing and accepted a tall glass from a plump girl in a spangled corset. She looked to Josh like one of old Harry Bosch's daughters. He shook his head. Pitt shrugged and drank. A thread of steam rose from the liquid when he lowered it. "I watched you as you came in. You don't approve of the renovations." It was a statement.

"I ain't used to seeing the place so gussy."

"The gameroom is unoccupied. I'll show it to you if you'll mosey in there with me." Laughing oddly, he rose. His coat-frock swayed, exposing briefly the shiny black handle of a Colt's Peacemaker strapped to his hip.

The side room was similarly appointed, with the addition of faro and billiard tables covered in red felt. Milton, the black stablehand's son, sat in the dealer's chair polishing a cuspidor.

"That will be all, lad." Pitt tossed him a silver dollar.

Josh laid a hand on Milton's shoulder as he was headed for the door. "Your pa know you're here?"

"No sir. I get a whuppin'. But Mr. Pitt he pays better than the hotel." He lowered his voice. "'Specially since he started paying real money." He left.

"Good lad. But I have hopes for him." Pitt took another sip and set his glass on the billiard table, where it boiled over.

"Who are you?" Josh asked.

"I am a speculator."

"Persephone's past speculating."

"That's where you're wrong, Marlowe. My commodity is most plentiful here."

"What's your commodity?"

"Something that is valued by only three in town at present. Milton's father Virgil, because he understands it. The half-breed Gordy Wolf, because he does not possess it. And I."

"What about me?"

"You have been a signal disappointment. When you came to this territory, that item which you are pleased to call yours was more than half mine. Since then you have begun to reclaim it."

"You came to take it back?"

Pitt laughed. It sounded like scales dragging over stone. "You exalt yourself. What is your soul against the soul of an entire town?"

"Then Virge and Gordy was right. You're him."

"Succinctly put. Gary Cooper would be proud."

"Who?"

"Perhaps I should explain myself. But where to start? Aha. Has it ever occurred to you in your wanderings that the people you meet are a tad too colorful, their behavior insufferably eccentric, their language over-folksy? That they themselves are rather—well, *broad*? Half-breed Crows tending bar, drunken college professors, henpecked merchants, gossipy blacksmiths, Negro liverymen who talk as if they just stepped off the plantation—really, where does one encounter these types outside of entertainment?"

"Keep cranking, Mr. Pitt. You ain't drawed a drop yet."

"There. That's just what I mean. Why can't you say simply that you don't follow? I don't suppose you'd understand the concept of alternate earths."

Josh said nothing.

"There is, if you will, a Master Earth, against which all the lesser alternate earths must be measured. Each earth has an equal number of time frames, and it's my privilege to move in and out of these frames among the Master and alternate earths. Now, on Master Earth, the American West within this frame is quite different from the one in which you and I find ourselves. This West, with its larger-than-life characters and chivalric codes of conduct, is but a mythology designed for escapist entertainment on Master Earth. That earth's West is a much drearier place. Are you still with me?"

"Sounds like clabber."

"How to put it." Pitt worried a whiskered lip between small ivory teeth. "You were a gunfighter.

Were you ever struck by the absurdity of this notion that the faster man in a duel is the moral victor, when the smart way to settle a fatal difference would be to ambush your opponent or shoot him before he's ready?"

"We don't do things that way here."

"Of course not. But on Master Earth they do. Or did. I get my tenses tangled jumping between time frames. In any case being who and what I am, I thought it would be fine sport to do my speculating in this alternate West. The fact that I am mortal here lends a nice edge to those splendid fast-draw contests like the one I enjoyed with Ned Harpy. His soul was already mine when I came here, but I couldn't resist the challenge." He sighed heavily; Josh felt the heat. "I'm aggrieved to say I've found none to compare with it. I'd expected more opposition."

"You talk like you got the town sewed up."

"I bagged the entire council this very afternoon when I promised them they'd find oil if they drilled north of Cornelius Street. The rest is sweepings."

"What do you need with Milton?"

"The souls of children hold no interest for me. But his father's would be a prize. I'm certain a trade can be arranged. Virgil will make an excellent pair of boots when these wear out." He held up a glossy black toe and laughed. Wind and rain lashed the windows, howling like demons.

"You trade *often?*"

Pitt cocked an eyebrow under the derby. "When the bargain is sufficient. What are you proposing?"

"I hear you're fast against saloonkeepers. How are you with a genuine gunman?"

"Don't be ludicrous. You haven't been in a fight in years."

"You yellowing out?"

Pitt didn't draw; the Peacemaker was just in his hand. Lightning flashed, thunder roared, a window-pane blew in the rain and wind extinguished the lamps in the room. All at once they re-ignited. The Peacemaker was in its holster. Pitt smiled. "What will you use for a gun?"

"I'll get one."

"That won't be necessary." He opened a drawer in the faro table and took out a glistening gray leather gun belt with a slate-handled converted Navy Colt's in the holster. "I think you'll find this will fit your hand."

Josh accepted the rig and drew out the pistol. The cylinder was full. "I sold this set in Tucson. How'd you come by it?"

"I keep track of such things. What are the spoils?"

"Me and the town if you win. If I win, you ride out on that red-eyed horse and don't come back. Leave the town and everybody in it the way you found them."

"That won't be necessary. In the latter event I'd be as dead as you in the former. In this world, anyway. What is hell for a gunfighter, Marlowe? Eternity on a dusty street where you take on all challengers, your gun hand growing swollen and bloody, never knowing which man you face is your last? I'll see you're kept interested."

"Stop jawing and go to fighting."

Smiling, Pitt backed up several paces, spread his feet, and swept his coat-frock behind the black-handled pistol, setting himself. Josh shot him.

The storm wailed. Pitt staggered back against the billiard table and slid to the floor.

Black blood stained his striped vest. The glass-blue eyes were wide. "Your gun was already out! You didn't give me a chance!"

Josh shrugged. "Did you think you were the only one who could travel between worlds?"

SWIFT JUSTICE AND LEGENDARY GUNSMOKE.

On October 26, 1881, nine men faced off in Tombstone, Arizona Territory, setting the stage for a clash that would echo through history. Within fifteen seconds, the street turned to dust as three men fell, their lives extinguished in a deadly showdown. The remaining six, including the legendary Wyatt Earp and the enigmatic Doc Holliday, survived to face trial—and kill again.

Bloody Season is an epic retelling of the infamous O.K. Corral shootout. Experience the raw, unfiltered brutality of the confrontation between Ike Clanton's cowboys and the Earp brothers by diving into the chaos, courage, and relentless spirit that defined one of the most storied battles of the Wild West.

AVAILABLE NOVEMBER 2024

ABOUT THE AUTHOR

Loren D. Estleman is the author of more than eighty novels and two hundred short stories, as well as articles and books of nonfiction on a wide variety of subjects. His historical novels include *Bloody Season*, based on events leading to and from the gunfight at the O.K. Corral; *This Old Bill*, about the life of Buffalo Bill Cody; *Aces & Eights*, tracing the career of Wild Bill Hickok; *The Ballad of Black Bart*, about the notorious stagecoach bandit; *The Eagle and the Viper*, dramatizing a plot to assassinate Napoleon Bonaparte; and novels based on the lives of Judge Isaac Parker, Judge Roy Bean, Pat Garrett and Billy the Kid, Al Capone, and Napoleon. He has been called the most critically acclaimed writer of his generation.

Estleman is also the author of the Amos Walker detective series. At forty-five years and thirty-three books, it's the longest-running single-author private eye series in publishing history. He has received more than twenty-five national awards, including three awards for lifetime achievement. He is a former Western Writers of America president and belongs to the Western Writers Hall of Fame. In 2002, Eastern Michigan University presented him with an honorary doctorate in Humane Letters. Estleman lives in Michigan with his wife, author Deborah Morgan.

BIBLIOGRAPHY